Cover Design: Jay Aheer
Editing done by Jenny Sims Editing4Indies
Proofing Julie Deaton by Deaton Author Services
Interior Design CP Smith

Titles by Natasha Madison

The Only One Series

Only One Kiss

Only One Chance

Only One Night

Only One Touch

Only One Regret

Only One Mistake

Only One Love

Only One Forever

Southern Series

Southern Chance

Southern Comfort

Southern Storm

Southern Sunrise

Southern Heart

Southern Heat

Southern Secrets

Southern Sunshine

This Is

This is Crazy

This Is Wild

This Is Love

This Is Forever

Hollywood Royalty

Hollywood Playboy

Hollywood Princess

Hollywood Prince

Something So Series

Something Series

Something So Right

Something So Perfect

Something So Irresistible

Something So Unscripted

Something So BOX SET

Tempt Series

Tempt The Boss

Tempt The Playboy

Tempt The Ex

Tempt The Hookup

Heaven & Hell Series

Hell And Back

Pieces Of Heaven

Love Series

Perfect Love Story

Unexpected Love Story

Broken Love Story

Faux Pas

Mixed Up Love

Until Brandon

ONLY ONE
Touch
THE ONLY ONE SERIES

ONE

BECCA

"BECCA," THE MALE caller says when he answers the phone.

"Mr. Grant," I say, tapping my Mont Blanc pen on my desk. I lean back in my office chair, looking out the window at the bright sun.

"You know shit is real when you call me Mr. Grant," Matthew says, and I laugh.

Sitting up straight in my chair, I say, "I'm wearing a different hat today. Usually when I call you, it's about making you pay more money." Matthew is the general manager for the New York Stingers, and as a sports agent, I have a couple of clients on his team. He comes from hockey royalty, so it's no surprise his son is following in his footsteps.

"How many hats do you wear?" he asks, and I have to smile. When it comes to my clients, I'll wear any hat I have to in order to earn them as much money and make them as successful as I can.

"I can't give away all my secrets." I remain my cool, calm, and collected self. "Today, my hat is that of an agent requesting a sit-down with the future NHL leading top scorer." Matthew listens without interrupting me because his son is the reason I'm calling. "I know Cooper will be drafted this year. He'll probably be number one if everything stays the same."

"Fingers crossed," Matthew says, and I can only imagine what he's going through as a parent not wanting his son to be compared to him. If anyone compared me to my mother, I think I would want the earth to swallow me up whole. "So what can I do for you, Becca?"

"I'm calling to see if you had time to meet with me. I'll be in New York at the end of next week," I say, looking at my calendar. I'll be in New York for four days.

"Should I be worried?" he asks, chuckling. "Every time you come to town, my salary cap goes up."

It's my turn to chuckle. "Come on, Matthew. We've known each other a long time. I've never been unfair to you."

"We can agree to disagree on this one," he says, and I can hear he's walking.

"Fair enough," I say, "but with that said, I'd love to sit down with Cooper and go over things to see if we are a good fit." He isn't going to get better than me. I also don't give him a chance to answer me. "I know that you want the best for Cooper, and bottom line, you have to admit"—I tap my perfectly manicured nail on the desk—"I'm the best."

I'm not going to beat around the bush anymore with him. I'm the best sports agent out there. Sure, people will try to argue how good I am, but I have the facts, and I have the numbers. I represent the top twenty leading players on the ice, not counting the other thirty scattered around. I've been hustling since day one to become the top female sports agent in the game, and now I'll fight to stay there.

He finally gives in. "I'll check our schedule and let you know when we're free." I'm about to push for something more definite when he adds, "I'll talk to Cooper tonight and see when is good for him and send you something."

"Sounds like a plan. I look forward to meeting with you two," I say, and we both hang up. I smile, knowing that the first step is getting them to the table to discuss what I can do for them. One thing I know how to do is sell myself.

Pulling my schedule out, I add him to the top of the list with a star to remind myself to reach out and give him a nudge if I don't hear back soon.

My phone pings, reminding me of our weekly meeting in the conference room in five minutes. I start to collect my papers and walk out of my corner office. "Erika," I say to my assistant, "you can leave early. Both of us don't have to suffer by staying."

"I just forwarded you the two emails we got this morning," she says. "I'll have my phone with me all weekend if something comes up." I nod, knowing she'll be ready to go regardless of what time I call her. She also has no idea I'm grooming her to become an agent. I know she has what it takes, and if she plays her cards right, she'll kill it.

Nothing screams good mood like Friday at four o'clock. "Have a nice weekend," I tell everyone who looks up at me as I walk toward the conference room.

I pass the receptionist, Tammy, who looks over at me and smiles. "Do you need anything, Becca?" she asks, and a smile fills my face.

"I would kill for a latte from Starbucks," I say, and she nods. I'm sure she has it ordered even before I walk into the conference room with the TRI Star Sports Agency logo decorating the wall.

Sitting in an empty seat, I'm about to page my two partners when they come walking into the room dressed almost identical. "Glad you two could join me," I say with a smirk. Francis winks at me, and I groan.

"She's your sister, asshole," Trevor says, sitting in the chair in front of me.

"Stepsister," Francis says, sitting down and grabbing a bottle of water from the middle of the table. "She's our stepsister, which makes her—" I sit back and cross my arms over my chest, looking at them.

"Off-limits," Trevor interrupts. "Bottom line, our father was married to her mother."

If you had told me when I was younger that these two would end up not only my best friends but also my business partners, I would have bet money against it. They came into my life when I was ten, and they were thirteen and fourteen, respectively.

My mother divorced my father when he had an affair with my nanny and my after-school tutor. To this day, I don't know if it was together or at different times. Don't feel too badly for my mother, though, because it took her less than a month to wrangle Ernest up, and they married in grand socialite style. She was the talk of the town, which she loved more than anything. She was the one woman to finally get Ernest to settle down after he lost his wife to breast cancer. He was raising his boys with the help of a nanny, a chef, a chauffeur, tutors, and anyone else he needed to hire to keep from spending time with them.

The three of us formed a bond like no other when the brothers were stuck dragging this annoying ten-year-old girl around with them. Our parents wed, and then they disappeared for a good six months. We had each other, and for seven years, it was what we thought our family would be. Our Christmases was spent skiing in Switzerland while our summers were on a yacht somewhere in Europe.

Everyone was living their best life until Ernest woke up one night with chest pains, and two hours later, he was pronounced dead, leaving my mother the grieving widow.

We each mourned differently. Francis went headfirst into sports. He was expected to be drafted first in the MLB until he tore his tendon in his knee the last game of the year.

Trevor buried his head in school and graduated with a master's degree in communication. I graduated with honors and went on to graduate with a master's degree in marketing.

On the other hand, my mother grieved by marrying another man, and this one had three kids. Luckily, we were all old enough not to have to be in each other's lives. It made it less messy when the divorce came. It's because of my mother that I don't think I will ever get married. I just don't want a man to have that kind of control over me.

"Okay," I say. "As much fun as it is watching you two go at it, I'd really love to get home before the sun goes down."

"I told Angelica that I would be home in time for dinner," Trevor says of his longtime girlfriend.

"I don't know how you do it." Francis looks at Trevor. "To be with the same one day in and day out." His face forms a grimace. When I graduated from the university, these two were the only ones cheering me on. Over beer and chicken wings, the three of us joked about starting a company with the chunk of change we inherited when Ernest died. No matter how many times I fought with them about giving it back, they refused to take it.

Francis got us our first client. It was someone he went to school with. His agent had just dropped him because of another DUI, and we decided that if we could turn his image around, it would look great for us. He then introduced us to other athletes, and slowly, but surely, we built our portfolio.

Francis takes care of baseball and golf. Trevor takes care of football. I take care of hockey, and we all split the basketball players.

We now have a staff of over one hundred, and we continue to grow every year.

"Okay, so what do we have going on this week?" I ask. They each fill me in on their prospects, and we finish the meeting in record time.

I walk back to my office and see that everyone has cleared out for the weekend. Grabbing my purse and laptop bag, I walk out just as the sun dips below the horizon.

I don't think I've left the office early in five years, I think as I'm unlocking my white Range Rover. I climb in and start it. My phone rings right away, and I look down to see Manning's name.

"It's Friday, and it's almost time for you to be at a dinner." Manning is the captain of the Dallas Oilers. The sponsors are all eating out of his hand because he stays out of drama. He refuses to be on social media other than his Facebook, where he pushes said sponsors.

"I'm on my way there now," he says.

"Good." I pull out of the parking lot. "I arranged for you to have a room downtown tonight in case you wanted to get a night away from the wicked witch of the east." I mention his wife that he refuses to leave.

He laughs. "I might take you up on that offer."

"Good," I say. "Call me tomorrow to let me know how the meeting went. Two other sponsors called me today. I'll research the companies and let you know."

"Sounds good," he says. "Have a great night." I disconnect at the exact time I pull up to my parking spot. I'm getting out when I get a text that makes my night.

Matthew Grant: Pencil us in for Friday afternoon. My office.

TWO

Nico

"WE HAVE A meeting in ten minutes with Frank," my assistant, Elizabeth, says from the doorway of my office. I look up and see her usual attire of a business suit with her hair in a high bun, and she's holding a leather folder in her hand. "If you leave now, you have seven minutes to eat before the meeting starts." Getting up, I look around the office at the sun shining in the sky and wonder what it would feel like to take a day off. But then I shake my head, reminding myself there is no time for that.

I walk out of the office and make my way down to the conference room. "Your mother called you," she says, opening her folder. "You have a meeting tonight at seven with the foundation chair," she says, going over my schedule.

When I inherited this team, the first thing I did was hire Elizabeth to be my right-hand person. We grew up together, and she's the only one I trust. As my nanny's daughter, the two of us were brought up almost like siblings. Only, she wasn't exploited because of who her parents were. "What's my weekend look like?"

"You have Candace's birthday party tomorrow," she tells me. "Gift is bought and already wrapped." I look over at her, and she smirks. "I got myself a matching one." We stop walking when we get to the doors of the conference room, and she smiles. "Your lunch is already in there. I have seven minutes, so I'm going to go outside and see if my skin glistens in the sun like a vampire." I shake my head, laughing at her. "I have my phone."

"I'm sure I can handle a meal without you, Lizzie." I use her nickname, and she rolls her eyes. Walking into the room, I see my brown paper bag at the head of the table right in front of the stack of papers we are going to go through. Slipping off my suit jacket, I put it over the back of the leather chair, then sit down and take out my sandwich. I grab my phone and get on my social media right away. I scroll through, seeing pictures of people on vacation. A couple of my old friends are partying in Vegas. I shake my head, taking another bite of the sandwich while trying not to remember what my life was like before.

I was the only son of oil tycoon John Earl Harrison the third and Daniella, an Italian model. They met at a fashion show in Milan. My mother got swept up with living the life in America. It was a whirlwind romance, and they wed at a venue with over one thousand guests just five months after they met. I can't even imagine the spectacle that was. They lived lavishly as jet-setters around the world, but always came back to Dallas, where the tabloids would be on full baby bump alerts. My mother knew she never really wanted children, but she had to give my father an heir. It was her duty as a wife to make sure his name lived on.

Thankfully, they got it right the first time and didn't have to go through it again. Every chance she got, she told me how I changed her body as she pointed out every stretch mark I gave her. The best thing they did for me was to hire Fernanda because she treated me like her own. It was usually just the two of us while my parents went away, which was most of the time. It's because of Fernanda I had a little bit of a normal upbringing. I was in every sport she could drive me to. My parents never attended any of the games because their schedules just didn't allow it.

My parents would take me out when the cameras were around, but Fernanda raised me. Slowly and quietly, I grew up. The press would follow me from time to time. Those embarrassing photos of me in college doing things I shouldn't be doing are floating around somewhere. I mean, everyone else did them, but I just got mine caught on camera. No one reported that I graduated with a bachelor's degree in economics and a master's degree in foreign communication.

They were on wedding watch as soon as I officially moved back to Dallas. It all became worse when my father gave me the Dallas Oilers. I was the youngest team owner ever. I had just turned thirty, and I had no idea what to expect. I knew what I didn't want, which was to be the laughing stock of the league. The team was a fucking mess. Even with our draft picks, they'd placed last in the league for seven years in a row. It was a shitshow.

Being twenty-seven and the owner of a professional sports team made me an eligible bachelor. The headlines were either Nicolas Edward Is dating so and so or Nicolas Edward just made another stupid trade.

I was over it all. It was almost like a downward spiral. I knew my father was waiting in the wings to swoop in and make it better, even if it was his fault that the team was so bad.

"Hey," Frank, the general manager for the team, says as he comes into the room with a coffee cup in his hand. "I thought I would be the early one."

I look at the phone and check the clock and see that he is two minutes early. I try not to roll my eyes at him and instead just nod. I'll wait until the meeting starts to get him in line. Frank has been with the team for the past seven years, and if you ask me, I would have fired him five years ago. But his contract is ironclad, so until it's up for renewal next year, I have no choice but to fucking keep him.

Grabbing my bottle of water, I drain it all, and I'm tossing it in the trash when Lizzie comes back with two cups of coffee in her hand. "Left," she tells me, so I know which coffee is mine. She nods at Frank and walks to the head of the table and takes a seat next to me.

The coach is the next to walk in. "Michel," I say to him, and he sits beside Lizzie. He has been my coach for the past two years. I got him when Montreal fired him.

Of course, Frank didn't want to hire him, but I give zero fucks what Frank thought about anything.

Usually, your general manager acquires the rights to player personnel by negotiating their contracts and reassigning or dismissing players no longer desired on the team. They may also have responsibility for hiring the head coach of the team. But not Frank. And not on my watch. It was rare to have an owner at the team meetings. It was also rare to have an owner negotiate the contracts, but I did. And sometimes I did it without even informing Frank, which didn't go over well with him. Again, I had zero fucks to give him.

"Okay, let's get this meeting started," I say, looking at my Rolex watch and seeing that it's precisely three on the dot. "We have a lot of ground to cover."

"How long is this meeting going to last?" Frank asks, and I look up at him. "It's a budget meeting, so I figured two hours tops."

"You are free to leave at any time," I say and then look over at Lizzie, who hands me the first file. "Six contracts will be expiring at the end of the season." I look down at the list and then back up. "Six that we need to keep."

"This wouldn't happen if you made me do my job," Frank says to me, and I lean back in my chair.

"Your job?" I laugh. "Was it your job to sign a thirty-seven-year-old to a six-year contract for forty-two million?" I ask. "The guy was one step to being retired." Frank just glares at me.

"He was a first round pick." He leans his arms on the table.

"When he was eighteen," I counter. "Let's look at this one. Kistoff." I open the file. "Another crazy fucking contract." I look down at it. "Five years for ten million, and he was thirty-five." I don't even bother letting Frank talk. "He had three fucking knee surgeries before he was signed."

"If you just play these guys …" he says, and Michel groans.

"Do you know how many times they had to sit out because they were hurt?" he asks Frank, and I just watch.

"You weren't even the coach," he spits at Michel.

"I didn't have to be the coach to know. There are very few who can skate at forty and make a difference."

"I agree," I say. "It's one thing to give them a one-year contract, but to sign them to these long contracts that I'm now stuck paying plus the ones I need. Which is why every fucking year I have to let go of players that I actually need."

"Oh, come on." His hand moves in the air.

"My father left you in charge," I say, "and trusted you, and what did you do?"

"It's not my fault." He shakes his head. "I'm not taking all the blame."

"You should," I say, and Michel nods his head.

"You're the one who put those contracts together. You're the one who hired every single player who was retiring. I don't even know what you were thinking."

"I was thinking that a man with experience could lead us to the Cup," he says.

"How do you think they are going to lead us to the

Cup if they can't fucking skate, Frank?" I shake my head and hold up my hand. "It's no secret that I'm not renewing your contract when it expires."

"I wouldn't want to stay here anyway," he says, making me laugh.

"Then why don't you leave now?" I say. "I mean, let's face it. You aren't doing anything."

"That's because you're a control freak who won't let me do my job!" he shouts, slamming his hand on the table. I think the fact that I'm cool, calm, and collected irritates him even more.

"That is because I sat down and read these contracts," I say. "You know the difference between my father and me?" I look at him, and he just glares at me. I know that as soon as he leaves here, he will call my father. He always does. "I give a shit. I want to win." I look at him. "I'm going to make sure that I build a team that has the same thirst for the Cup as I do."

He stands from his chair and looks at me. "You didn't work for this team," he says. "It was handed to you."

"What was handed to me was a pile of shit," I say. "But I'm going to turn that pile of shit into gold." He laughs at me and walks out of the room. I look around the table. "Just so we're clear, if you aren't here to fight to get to number one, then you should leave now." I look around the room and then look at Lizzie, who smirks. I clap my hands together. "Let's get to work."

THREE

BECCA

THE SWEAT POURS off me as I run on the treadmill, looking out the window in my home gym as the sun slowly rises. It's my thing to get up every day at five thirty, no matter where I am, and run for at least an hour. It clears my head. I also come up with the best ideas while on this fucking treadmill.

The television plays in the background as I make my list of notes. The beep of the treadmill lets me know I'll be slowing down. My running goes from full speed to a slow jog, giving my breathing a chance to return to normal as I cool down. I grab my water bottle and finish it as the treadmill comes to a stop. Grabbing my towel, I wipe the sweat away from my face as I make my way to my bedroom. The penthouse was the first real big thing I bought for myself. It set me back close to ten million, but it was just what I wanted.

The two-floor penthouse has floor-to-ceiling windows

in every room, providing a lot of natural light. I head into my bathroom, opening the shower door and starting the water while I peel off my sports bra and black shorts. Stepping into the massive shower, I let the water run over my long brown hair as I wash.

When I step out, I slip on my terry cloth robe and wrap my hair up to walk to the kitchen. The kitchen is all white with black marble countertops. The stainless-steel appliances are not used that much since I'm rarely home. I think the only time I use the stove is on Saturday and Sunday. The fridge is always fully stocked, thanks to my cleaning lady who comes in twice a week. I start the Nespresso coffee machine, then grab my milk and pour some in. Going back to the fridge, I pick up the turkey sausage and a couple of eggs to start my breakfast while I drink my coffee. I'm taking out the stuff for my shake when my phone rings, and I grab it without looking at the name.

"Hello," I say, looking over at the clock to see what time it is. It's just after eight—early for a Saturday morning—so that could only mean one thing. Shit is going down somewhere.

"Becca, it's Adrian." I stop moving in my kitchen when I hear the voice of Adrian Kirkpatrick, publicist to five of my clients. He sounds out of breath. I can tell he's either walking somewhere or running. It's only six where he is, so he was definitely woken up.

"This better be a fucking wellness check," I say, but my stomach tells me otherwise. I turn on *SportsCenter* right away to see if I missed something.

"I'm on my way to bail out Andrei," he says, and I close my eyes as I hear his car starting.

"What happened now?" I ask. I know I'm not going to like how this conversation ends.

"He was caught speeding on the I-9. When they searched him, he had cocaine on him, and when they tried to detain him, he assaulted the officer."

"For the love of fucking Christ," I say, putting my head down. The towel falls off my head, and I put the call on speaker. "I'm done."

"Oh, come on, Becca," Adrian huffs out, and I can almost see his face. "It's not that big of a deal."

"Not that big of a deal?" I repeat, my voice staying calmer than the rage coursing through my body. "Not that big of a deal would be him being cited for jaywalking. Possession and assault are totally a huge fucking deal." I raise my hands in the air and shake them.

"I admit, it isn't going to look good," Adrian concedes, and I roll my eyes, "but I think we can put a spin on it."

"Spin it?" I ask, but I'm really not asking. "You can't be serious."

"I am. This can be him starting over. People will relate to him." I don't think this will ever happen. I don't tell him that the only thing anyone will wonder is how many times we can give this guy a chance.

"You can do whatever you like," I say. "My office is going to be issuing a statement that we are parting ways and wishing him well." I grab my phone and text my brothers that we have a problem.

"How is that going to look on your side?" he says, and I chuckle.

"It's going to look like we don't stand for this shit. We aren't going to condone this behavior. It doesn't matter who you are or what you bring in. Our company has a name to uphold and an image to protect, and having this isn't something I want—"

"Just like that?" Adrian cuts me off.

"Just like fucking that," I say. "I stood by his side when he crashed not one but two cars and entered rehab. I stood by his side when he beat the shit out of his girlfriend, and I had two of his three sponsors pulling their contracts. This is strike three." I shake my head. "I warned him the last time, and you were there. I will not be here to clean up his mess. That is what he pays you to do."

"I'm sorry you feel that way," he says. "I'll tell Andrei when I see him."

I disconnect the call and then call my brother Trevor, knowing that Francis is probably still sleeping. "How is it that you have drama at eight o'clock on a Saturday morning?"

"I'm dropping Andrei as a client," I say, and he listens as I fill him in. "I'll call Amanda now so she can issue a press release." I mention our public relations director.

"Yeah, I would do the same," he says. "You tried and stuck by him when no one else did."

"I'm going to wish him well and move on," I say. "Now I have to go eat my breakfast and try not to dwell on it." I tie my wet hair on top of my head again. "I'll send you a copy of the letter once I'm finished with it."

My morning flies by as well as the afternoon, dealing with the aftermath of Andrei. His arrest is front and center at noon, the same time we release our statement. I rub my hands over my face and look down to see that I'm still in my robe and my breakfast is still sitting there but cold. I throw it out and grab one of the pre-made foods I have delivered. I pop it in the microwave to heat it faster and eat standing up this time, not bothering to move from the kitchen when my phone pings. I groan when I see it's a reminder for tonight.

Candace's birthday party

Putting my head back, I can sense a headache coming on. I finish my food and make my way to my bedroom. My bed calls my name, and I finally listen to it and crawl into my bed naked. It takes me no time to fall asleep, and when the alarm rings two hours later, I almost send Ralph a message that I'm going to bail, but I know I have to make an appearance.

Dragging my ass out of bed, I head into my walk-in closet to get dressed. It's the size of a bedroom with clothes on all four walls sorted by color and then by designer. I pick out tight black pants that fit me like a glove and a black lace halter top with a tight black jacket cut down in the front to show the lace under it. I set the clothes down on the bed and go into the bathroom and curl my hair. I have my hair and makeup done in thirty minutes, and I get a text telling me the car will be here in ten minutes.

I slip on my clothes and then walk over to my shoes,

grabbing a pair of gold Louboutins. My feet scream at me for putting them through this torture. "It hurts to be beautiful." Grabbing my black Hermes purse, I walk out of the penthouse and make my way down to the waiting car.

The driver opens the door as soon as he sees me. I usually drive, but I figured that I could have a couple of drinks. "Thank you," I say, getting into the car. I spend the drive over scrolling through Instagram and see a couple of pictures from my clients that I like.

When we pull up to the restaurant, I put the phone back in my purse, and the driver comes over and opens the door. "I'll be waiting right here when you are ready."

"Thank you," I say and walk into the restaurant. The whole place is shut down just for us. People are lingering everywhere, and I look around, spotting Candace and Ralph talking to Miller and Layla. I make my way over and see balloons scattered around the room. "Happy Birthday," I say when I get close enough to them. Candace looks up and smiles at me. She is a sought-after social media specialist. I met Ralph three years ago when he first got traded to Dallas, and he had no agent. I signed him after meeting with him for five minutes. He was genuine and down to earth, and then his whole life turned upside down.

"Becca," Candace says, coming over to me, "I got your bracelet." She shows me the Cartier one I bought her. "It's stunning and so thoughtful."

"It was my pleasure," I say, and I show her the same one on my wrist next to my gold Rolex. "I saw you looking at it the last time we were together."

"Yeah, thanks for that," Ralph says. "Made the brace-let I got her look lame."

I laugh. "Oh, please." I walk to Ralph and kiss his cheek and then do the same to Miller and Layla. Miller is another one of my clients. He's the it boy on the ice, Mr. GQ they call him, and was the most eligible bachelor before Layla got her hooks into him. Now they could parade a whole harem of women in front of him, and he wouldn't even bat an eyelash. "Where is Manning?" I ask of the third person in their trio.

"His son had a hockey game or something," Miller says. "I think it was an excuse not to hang around with Murielle." We all laugh. He's kept it a huge secret that he's been trying to get divorced for the past four years, and she refuses to grant him one. She actually took their son and ran away when he served her with papers the first time.

"Anyone care for some champagne?" the server asks us, and I smile, grabbing a glass.

"To Candace," I say. Holding up my glass, I add, "And to the two guys who do what they're told."

"Cheers," everyone says, and I take a sip of the cham-pagne.

"Let's grab our seats," Layla says to us, and we walk to sit down at the table.

When I sit next to one of the rookies, who smiles at me, I groan inwardly and think *here we go.*

FOUR

Nico

I PARK MY BMW SUV in an empty parking spot, then get out and walk to the restaurant. I've been on the go since five this morning. I spent three hours working out all the frustration I had from yesterday.

The meeting lasted five hours yesterday. We picked it up again today for another four hours, but I think we finally found a way to get the expiring contracts signed without going over my cap. I pull open the door to the restaurant and look around. The restaurant is closed just for us, which is something we always have to do to enjoy our time.

I stop as soon as I walk in, shaking one of the guy's hands. I look around then to see if I can spot Ralph, who is right beside Candace. "Happy Birthday," I say, handing her the gift Lizzie bought.

"Great," Ralph says. "You walk in looking all *GQ*." I look down at my outfit. After being in a suit last night and knowing that I have to wear one tomorrow, I opted to wear blue jeans with a white button-down shirt and a blue cashmere sweater over it.

"We're dressed the same," I say, looking at his outfit.

"Whatever," he says and then points at the gift. "I already know you spent too much on this." He shakes his head.

"To be honest," I say, "Lizzie is the one who bought the gift, and she bought herself one also."

"Ohh," Candace says, "maybe it's diamond earrings." She tries to look in the bag. "Lizzie always has the best taste in everything."

"If that contains diamond earrings, you are giving it back," Ralph says, and I just laugh. "I'm not kidding."

"Okay, I'm going to leave you two to handle whatever it is you are handling," I tell them and walk away. The two of them are perfect for each other. When I found out they were together, I wasn't at all shocked because they really are a perfect couple. Whenever I see them, it makes me wonder if I will ever find that person who completes me. Is true love really a thing? But I don't really have time for love. I don't have time to wine and dine someone. Do I date? I mean, generally, I slip my dates between my business meetings. But no woman wants to come second to my job. And my job is always going to be my priority.

I stop to talk to a couple of people before I make my way over to Becca. I can hear chatter all around me, but as I get closer to her table, I hear her voice now.

"So what you are saying," Becca says, setting down

her champagne glass, "is that my stocks in my company are going to go up if you take me as your agent?" I stop in my tracks and watch as the rookie smirks at her.

"Yes," he says. "I'm up and coming, and if everything goes according to plan, I'll be in demand." I hold my breath.

"Let me just fill you in on something," she says, turning so she can see him face-to-face. "My stock is already skyrocketing, and it has nothing to do with you or whatever you think you bring to the table. Which, as of right now, are only empty promises," she tells him.

He opens his mouth to speak when she puts up her hand. "Furthermore, I'm going to let you in on a little secret. Deflate that ego of yours just a bit more because, in one shift, you can be yesterday's news. With that said, I think I'm going to pass on the offer to be your agent." She turns around, leaving David with his mouth hanging open as she picks up her glass of champagne and drains it.

"Well, then," he says, getting up, "good talking to you."

She smiles at him, and I step up before she chews him up and spits him back out. "Hey," I say, walking up. Becca looks up at me, and I have to say I don't think I've ever noticed how beautiful she is. Her green eyes are almost the color of an emerald. "Becca," I say, sitting in the chair in front of her. "David," I say, and he nods at me before walking away. "That was …" I say, shaking my head. "I think he's going to cry."

She rolls her eyes. "You would not believe the shit he

said," she says and smiles at the waiter who replaces her empty glass with a full one. "Thank you." I see that her eyes lighten up just a touch when she smiles. "You think I was too hard on him?"

I've known Becca ever since I became the owner and showed up at her first meeting with us. We've gone toe-to-toe before, and we can both be cutthroat for the people we believe in. Usually, we are on the same page, and even though we've disagreed, we've always stayed professional. "He needed that," I say of David. "His numbers lead him to believe he's invincible on the ice, and that can be dangerous."

"Well, you know what they say. The higher up you are, the harder you fall," she says. "Sorry." Shaking her head, she leans forward, and I see lace under her jacket. And for the first time in I don't know how long, I find I'm interested in seeing what else is under her jacket. "It's been a day."

"Don't I know it," I say and put my hand up for the waiter. When he comes over, I order a beer.

"Whoa," she says, and I look at her.

"I don't think I've ever seen you drink at an event," she says, and I lean back in my chair. "Usually, it's a bottle of water."

"I've spent a whole week going over my budget," I say. She leans forward, and I smell citrus.

"You don't need a beer," she says. "You need a bottle of scotch."

I laugh, knowing she's right. "I've never heard you laugh."

"That's because every time I sit down with you, I feel you squeeze …" I'm about to say my balls, but something stops me. "My neck."

Her laughter sends shivers up my arms. "Oh, come on. It's not that bad." She drinks more of her champagne, and I wonder if her lips taste sweet. It's only when I have that thought do I stop staring at her. Where the fuck is all this coming from? I'm afraid to say anything with the direction of my thoughts. "I let you win sometimes." She hides her smile with her champagne glass.

"Sometimes." I shake my head, hoping to clear out the idea of her naked in front of me. "And then sometimes …"

"And sometimes it feels like I'm kicking you in the ass." She tilts her head slightly to the side, smiles, and then shrugs. "It might be why I'm good at my job."

"Without a doubt," I say. "I've sat with many agents." I grab the beer bottle and bring it to my lips, taking a pull before I choose my next words. The coldness of the beer hits my tongue.

"Wait," she says, holding up her hands before I continue talking. "If you are going to give me a compliment, I'm going to tape it and then write it on my calendar." My head goes back, and I swear I haven't laughed that hard in forever.

"Now it's my turn to say I'm not that bad." I look at her.

"The last time we sat down in your conference room, you called me egotistical," she says. It takes me a second to go through my memory and find that moment. I'm shocked by just how many memories I have of her.

"I'm sure I didn't say those exact words." I roll my lips when she gasps.

"I believe your exact words were come down out of the clouds, Becca, and stop being so fucking egotistical." She points at me. "Okay, maybe not exactly, but you definitely called me egotistical."

"What are you two laughing about?" Miller says, pulling out the seat beside me and sitting down. Layla walks over to the other side of the table, pulling out her own chair and sitting next to Becca. I watch Becca turn and look over, smiling as her hair falls forward. My hand itches to reach over and move it so I can see her eyes.

"We are talking about the last time Nico paid me a compliment and called me egotistical," she tells Miller.

"Oh, I remember that," Miller says, snapping his fingers.

"No, you don't." I shake my head, rolling my eyes.

"No, I do," he says, looking at Layla. "I was there. You two were discussing my contract." He then looks at me. "You were pissed with her demands. I thought the vein in your head was going to explode. You called her egotistical." He laughs. "Becca didn't even bat an eyelash. All she did was shrug and tell you she's been called worse."

"Yes," Becca says, slapping the table. "I knew I was right." Her laughter is contagious, making me smile. "We should have bet."

"I was not that heated," I point out, and Miller looks at me in shock.

"Dude," he says, "let's just say that day I was happy I was on Becca's side of the table."

I roll my eyes. "It was not that fucking bad," I say.

"That's okay," Becca says, leaning over the table and putting her hand on mine. I think she's done this before. In fact, I know she's done this before. But now her warm, soft hand on mine feels like an electric shock going through my body, zapping my brain. "I really have been called worse." She leans back in her chair, taking her hand off mine. "One owner called me a swingy scummy wormy bitch." I look at her with my mouth open as she laughs about it.

"What did you do?" Layla asks, intrigued as much as I am.

"I smiled at him, and then the next day, I sent him a box of worms." The three of us laugh so loud people look over at our table.

"So this is where the party is happening," Ralph says, pulling up a chair and sitting at the table with us. "What did Miller do this time?" he asks, and his question has merit since Miller is usually the one making us laugh. I watch Becca as Miller fills Ralph in. The little sparkle in her eye makes her eyes look gold on the bottom and green on the top.

The waiter comes over and grabs her empty glass, and when he goes to put another one down, she shakes her head. She turns and catches me watching her. "Did you drive here?" I ask her, and she shakes her head.

"No," she says, leaning forward. Her jacket opens just a bit, and even though about fifty people are here, my eyes are only on hers. It feels as if we are the only ones in the room. "I have a strict two-drink maximum."

I cock my head to the side. "Really?" I lean forward. "Is there a reason?"

"Well, besides the fact that no good choices are made when one drinks?" She smiles and winks at me, and I can only imagine what bad decisions she's talking about. But I know one thing—I will be finding out exactly how bad these decisions are.

FIVE

BECCA

"WELL, BESIDES THE fact that no good choices are made when one drinks?" I smile at him, which I'm doing a lot tonight, then I wink at him. Holy shit, am I flirting with him? Wait a second, why am I flirting with him? What is going on right now?

"You've got to give me something better than that," he says, and I look at him. I mean, really look at him, and it's like I'm seeing him for the first time. His brown hair is long on top and short on the sides and the back, and it looks like it took him two seconds to run his fingers through it. His blue eyes get a bit lighter when he laughs, almost like the amber of cognac. When he leans forward on the table, his biceps flex under his blue sweater.

"Ugh." I throw my head back. "Why?"

"Because I don't think I've ever seen you make one bad decision since we've been in business with each other." I tilt my head to the side, looking over at Miller and

Layla, who are holding hands across the table. Ralph has pulled Candace onto his lap and is whispering something in her ear. "So tell me," Nico says, and I turn my attention back to him. "Give me one example."

"Oh, God." I think about it for a second. "But if you ever throw this in my face, I will …" I point at him, and he holds up his hands and crosses it over his chest.

"Scout's honor," he says, smirking.

"You were never a scout, Nico." I lean back in my chair and cross my legs. "Fine. Four months ago, I went to a Celine Dion concert," I tell him, and I can see his eyes change color to a soft blue. "I had a couple more vodka drinks than I should have, and well …" I put my head down. "I can't show anyone the videos because all you hear is my screaming and singing in the background."

He laughs, clapping his hands together. "I would never peg you for a Celine fan."

"Yeah, well, I wish that was the worst of it," I say, and I suddenly wish I didn't have a two-drink limit that I stick by, especially at a work function. It's one thing to enjoy a bottle of wine at home on my couch, but it's another thing to do it in front of my clients. "The next morning, I woke up …" I lean forward, and I see his eyes go back to a darker blue. "Naked. Next to me was a black baseball cap with diamonds all over it with the word BOSS across it." He rolls his lips to stop from laughing. "I even have a picture," I say, grabbing my phone and opening up my photos to search for it. I find it on my Instagram and show it to him.

He takes my phone from me, and our fingers graze each other. And just like before when he put his hand on mine, a shiver goes up my spine. He looks at the picture, and he zooms in. "That hat is very …"

"Shiny?" I say. "Bright?"

"You ever try to wear this hat out in the sun?" he asks, and I shake my head and laugh.

"They should not allow you to buy merchandise after the show." I point at him. "Especially if you buy more than one thing."

"What else did you buy?" he asks.

"A T-shirt, mug, calendar, a sweater, and a poster," I say, and he is trying so hard not to laugh. "It's not funny."

"I'm just wondering where you hung the poster. Is it in your bedroom or office?" he asks, and I flip him the bird. I see him doing a couple of things with his fingers.

"What are you doing?" I ask, and he hands me back my phone.

"I followed myself on Instagram," he says, and I look down to see that he also requested to follow me. When I look back up, he has his phone in his hand. "You can accept now."

"We'll see," I say, putting my phone away, and he glares at me.

"Whatever you say, boss," he says, and it's my turn to glare at him. This time, his eyes turn almost a grey when he laughs. He holds up his hands. "I was kidding."

"I'll remember that the next time you ask me for something," I say, and he shakes his head.

"Well, this was fun," I say. We are the only two left

at the table while everyone else mingles. "I'm going to head out."

He looks at me. "I can drive you," he says, getting up, and my eyes fly down to his zipper. That is the first time in my life I've ever done that. I whip my head up so fast that I have to hold on to the table. "You okay?" he asks, and I wonder if he caught me staring at his package. I'm so distorted by this that I forget to tell him that I already have a ride home.

"Yeah," I say. "My foot was asleep," I lie to him as we make our way over to Ralph and Candace. We say goodbye to them, and I feel the heat of his hand on my lower back coming through my jacket. We walk out of the restaurant, and the cool air hits us.

"This was really nice," he says, his hand still on my back, and I stop at the entrance of the restaurant. "Like really nice," he says, and he's looking at me differently.

I hold my purse with both my hands, and I tuck a strand of hair behind my ear. I'm suddenly fucking nervous, and I have no idea what is going on. Maybe the champagne was not good or spiked.

"I haven't had this much fun in a long, long time," I say. He leans closer to me, and I don't know why my heartbeat speeds up. Or why my hands get clammy or why my stomach feels like it's a fish out of water flopping all over the place.

"Well, since Celine," he whispers. I go to push him with my hand, and he grabs it. "I'm kidding," he says. Standing really fucking close to him, I look up at him, and even with my heels, he's still taller than my five-foot-seven frame. I never realized how tall he was before.

Both of us stand here, not saying anything when a car pulls up. "That's for me," I say, looking at the driver getting out of the car and coming over to open the door for me. "Thank you, Nico," I say, leaning in and kissing him on the cheek. The musky smell of him hits me right away. "For the laughs."

"You are most welcome, Becca," he says, and I step away from him and walk toward the waiting car. "Oh, and, Becca?" He calls my name just as I get to the car door. I turn to look at him over my shoulder, putting one hand on the door. "Your secret is safe with me." He smirks. "Boss."

I throw my head back and laugh while I flip him the bird. "Have a nice night, Nico," I say, ducking and getting into the car.

I wait for the driver to close the door before I let out the deep breath I was holding in. I put my hand on my stomach as I look forward and see the driver climb into the car. I don't look out my window, but I feel his eyes on me. As we pull away from the curb, I turn to see that he is watching the car drive off.

I look out the window the whole time on the way to my penthouse. "Don't get out," I say when we pull up out front. Opening the door, I get out and walk into the lobby. The security guard gets up to walk me to the elevator. "Have a great night, Robert," I say when I get into the elevator.

I slip out of my shoes as soon as I close the door behind me and walk up the steps to my bedroom using only the moonlight to guide my way. My phone beeps from my purse. I turn on the light as I toss my purse on the couch in front of my bed.

Sitting down, I take the phone out and see it's a text from Nico.

Nico: If I sing "My Heart Will Go On", will you accept my follow request on Instagram?

I laugh, going to my walk-in closet and taking a picture of me wearing the hat. I bend down so he can only see the top of the hat and not my face. I send him the picture, and it takes him two seconds to answer me.

Nico: That is going to be my screen saver.

I laugh, shaking my head.

Me: Have a nice night, Nico.

I put down the phone and undress. After tossing the clothes into the wash, I go to bed. The next morning when I'm on the treadmill, I get a message from Manning.

Manning: Call me when you're up.

I press call, and he picks up right away. "How are you up? It's like six in the morning."

"Is that what you wanted me to call you about?" I ask, huffing out, turning the speed of the treadmill down in case I have to talk.

"I was wondering if we could schedule a meeting," he says, and I worry something is wrong. His tone is tight, and I immediately stop my treadmill. My heart beats fast, and it's not because I'm running.

"Are you in trouble?" I ask. I'm ready to help him in any way he needs it. Manning was the first big name to sign with me. He was the first one to take a chance on me, and I will never forget it.

"It's nothing serious," he says, and his voice goes low. "I mean, it's serious, but I will explain later tonight if I can."

"Come over whenever you want. I'm home all day and night," I say.

"Okay, I'll call you before I head over," he says. We hang up, and the whole day I'm on pins and needles. When he shows up after eight that night, he looks ragged.

"What in the hell happened to you?" I ask, and I can see he is going through something.

"Can we sit down?" he asks. I nod, leading him into the penthouse and gesturing to the couch.

"Okay," I say, sitting in front of him. "You are really scaring me."

"I want to leave Murielle," he says of his wife.

"Okay, we can do that. I have the best divorce lawyer on speed dial," I say. "We dated for maybe a week."

"It's not that easy," he says. "Last time I did that, she ran away with Jax." He mentions his son. "And the only way she would come back is if I promised not to bring up divorce again." He looks down and then up. "I met someone," he says, and I see the anguish all over his face. "It hasn't been long, but in this short time, I know I don't want to let her go."

"I don't know what to say," I say, sitting next to him.

"Murielle is having an affair with her trainer, and I have all the proof from the house camera." My mouth opens in shock. "And I could blackmail her with it, but then …" He shakes his head. "I don't want to use those pictures of her in my house."

"We need to hire a private investigator to follow her and snap the pictures," I say, getting up to get my phone.

"You have one of those on speed dial?" he asks, and I look at him.

"What do you think?" I send the private eye a message. "I have everyone screened before I sign them." He just stares at me. "If there is anything out there, this guy is going to find it."

"I trust you," he says, and I nod at him.

"What are you going to do with the evidence?" The question is a loaded one.

"I'm going to get my life back." The struggle in his voice is apparent.

"Well, Manning, I hope you got your gear on because we are about to go to war," I say. "And I'm not about to lose to that bitch."

SIX

Nico

"WE LEAVE TOMORROW," Lizzie says from across the desk. "The team is in Buffalo." We've been in my office all day going over contracts since I walked in at ten this morning. The only thing I've done is taken off my jacket and rolled up my sleeves.

"How long are we in Buffalo?" I ask, not sure anymore of the travel schedule. I go to every single away game and make sure to work my schedule around it. I don't go when the team goes. Instead, I fly out for the game, and sometimes I'll fly back with them if they are coming right back. There have been times when I follow the team, and Lizzie hates every second of it.

"For two days," she says. "Then we go on the road with them to New York." I lean back in my big leather chair and rock. The office I'm in was never used before. It was my father's office, but he never stepped foot in it. When I got the team, I changed almost everything to get rid of the coldness and the emptiness of the office. I had the team sign a jersey, and I had it framed and hung on the wall in here. I then started adding pictures here and there. One from the time we played in the Winter Classic. There is a picture of me standing in the middle of the owner's box with my back to the camera as I looked out at the crowd. It was the first time the arena ever sold out, and it's my most prized possession.

"You can opt out if you want," I say, and she looks at me with her eyebrows raised.

"You know damn well that I would never say no to going to New York." She taps her pen. "What's wrong with you?" She leans back in her chair, and I just look at her. "You've been strange this week."

"It's Wednesday," I say, "so technically, it hasn't been a week." She eyes me, and I can see all her questions. She's legit my best friend, but I don't even know how to say what I'm feeling. Even I have to admit it's been a weird fucking week. I'm thinking of Becca more and more, and I have no fucking reason. I'm about to say something when my receptionist comes into the room with a box.

"You got a package." She walks to me with the big white box in her hands and sets it on my desk. "And it's heavy."

"You know what they say about heavy packages," Lizzie says, and I look over at her as she looks at the box. "Not worth the hype."

"I've heard and seen that before," my receptionist says, then walks out of the room.

"Are you going to open the package, or are you going to make me spend the day guessing what is inside and who sent it?" I look down at the white box with the big red silk bow. "That looks like a sex box." I look up at her, shaking my head.

"What?" I ask, shocked. "How?"

"Red means sex," she says as if it's actually a thing.

"Who said that, and how do you even know this?" I look back down at the big white box and pick up the end of the red silk ribbon.

"A bunch of reasons." She holds her hand up to count off the reasons. "One, the red room. It was legit a room for kinky sex," she says, putting up one finger. "Two, red bottom shoes. You think those shoes were created for anything but sex? No woman in the universe will tell you those shoes were made for comfort." I sit here, my mouth hanging open in shock, wondering what the fuck she is talking about. "Three, wearing red lipstick."

"That means sex?" I ask, pinching my eyebrows together.

"Put your red lipstick on my dipstick." She shakes her head, laughing. "Now, can you please show me what the heck is in the box?" She gets up and comes over to my big desk.

I slip the red bow off and slowly open the top of the box. I don't know why I'm suddenly scared of what is inside. A white envelope sits on top, and folded white tissue paper means you can't see what is underneath it. My name's written on the front in neat handwriting.

"That's a woman's writing," Lizzie says. "A woman sent you a gift?" She gasps and puts her hand to her mouth. "You hooked up with someone." She puts her hands on her hips, and she doesn't give me a chance to answer her. "Why didn't you tell me? When was this? Where was this? The only place you went all weekend was to Candace's birthday party." She glares. "Did you have sex with a waitress?"

"Would you simmer down. It could be the clerk who wrote it," I inform her. "It doesn't mean that a woman sent me this."

"Okay, so what does it say?" She folds her arms over her chest. When I open the letter, I could swear it smells like Becca. The smell of citrus and a hint of something else.

Turning it over, I slip the envelope flap open and pull the note out. I read the note, and I throw my head back and laugh. Putting the note on top of the envelope, I place it right beside the white box. I open the white tissue paper, and the bottle of scotch is in the middle of the box with two glasses. Items all around it are wrapped in white tissue paper.

"Nico, I thought this would make you smile. Enjoy the scotch. Thanks for the laughs." I look up and see Lizzie's face. "Becca?" She looks at me. "Like Becca Becca?"

"Can you relax, please," I say, opening another white tissue and seeing a Celine Dion calendar.

"Like the Becca who is supermodel beautiful with perfect hair and a kick-ass body? That Becca?" I look at her, trying to hide the fact that I think of her as all that and just a bit more. "Oh, come on, you had to have noticed how beautiful she is. This is not new information to anyone. Last time she was here, the valet guy tripped and brought her the wrong car."

"She is beautiful," I admit out loud to Lizzie, and I wonder why I haven't noticed before this weekend. Maybe I did notice, but I didn't want to admit it. It might have just been the fact we were just sitting together as two people at a friend's party without the stress of going toe-to-toe.

"Celine Dion." She takes the calendar out of my hand, turning it over to check the pictures on the back. I pick up a wrapped roll, and when I peel the tissue off, it's a Celine T-shirt. The laughter escapes me. "Do you even like Celine?" Lizzie asks when she spots the T-shirt with Celine's face.

"I mean, I never really thought about it," I answer honestly. I take out the last wrapped package, and this time, I throw my head back and belly laugh.

"That's a whole lot of bling," Lizzie says of the boss hat in my hand. "You can't wear that outside in the sun." I can't stop laughing at the hat.

It really was a bad decision. I'm about to pick up my phone and call her when it rings. "Hello?" I say in the phone, and I hear the team trainer, Richard.

"Nico." His voice is low. "There was an accident on the ice."

I sit up, the hat falling from my hands back into the white box. "What type of injury and who?"

I get up and look over at Lizzie, who is already on her

phone, her fingers flying across the keyboard. She grabs her leather folder and zips it closed as she follows me out of my office. "It's Brendan." I stop walking. Brendan is one of the top scorers on the team. I got him in a trade with Washington two years ago.

"How bad?" I walk out of the office with Lizzie behind me. I can hear her murmuring to someone on her phone.

"Bad," he says. "We are on our way to the hospital."

"What the fuck happened?" I ask, my voice tense.

"He was moving up the ice, and I don't know what the fuck happened. He must have moved bad or something. He said he heard a pop."

Pressing the button to the elevator, I ask, "What do you think it is?"

"One of the doctors here thinks it's his ACL," he says, and I close my eyes. An ACL can have you out anywhere from six months to a year.

"The plane will be ready in thirty," Lizzie says from beside me.

"I'll be flying out in thirty minutes," I say and rush home to pick up my packed bag. You only have to be stuck without clothes once to always have a bag ready to leave. It takes me ten minutes to get home, and I park right outside the door. I take the elevator up to the third floor instead of the stairs. It might not be faster, but my nerves are all over the place.

Walking into my walk-in closet, I grab the packed black bag and head back downstairs. "I'm ready," Lizzie says, meeting me in the foyer. My house is huge. It has three floors with a walkway connecting the main house to the two-bedroom apartment over the three-car garage on the other side of the property, which is where she lives. "Any news?"

"He's getting an MRI right now," I tell Lizzie as we get into the car taking us to the airport.

We take off as soon as I'm buckled in, and my phone beeps that he is still in with the doctor. We land in Buffalo three hours later, and a SUV is waiting to take us to the hospital.

My finger taps my phone, waiting for it to ring. "No news is good news," Lizzie says from beside me.

"I hope to fuck it's not bad news," I say once we pull up to the hospital. I get out and find Patrick, the team doctor, in the waiting room. "So what's the verdict?" I ask, and I can see from his eyes it's not fucking good.

SEVEN

BECCA

I STEP OUT of the elevator just after nine in the morning with a Starbucks in one hand and my tan Hermes bag in the other. "Good morning," I tell the receptionist, who smiles at me.

"I love your look today," she says. "Very casual chic."

"That's what I was going for," I say of the light pink tight pants that reach just to my ankles and a silk flowy long-sleeved leopard print top tucked in. My shoes match the color of my pants. "Anything for me?" I ask, and she hands me my mail.

I smile at her and pretend it doesn't bother me that Nico hasn't acknowledged the gift I sent him yesterday. I don't know what I was expecting, but I wasn't expecting radio silence. *What do you want from him?* I don't know, maybe I thought Saturday meant something. I thought I felt something, but maybe it was all in my head.

"Good morning," I tell everyone I see when I walk in.

"Hey," I say to Erika my assistant. "How are you?"

"Good," she says, looking up at me and standing to follow me into my office. "I don't want to say anything to jinx us," she says, and I look at her when I get to my desk, "but nothing is happening."

I put down my coffee and mail. "I don't even know how to handle that."

"I know, I came in this morning, and there were four emails. *Four*."

"Is the server down?" I ask and then yell for Francis. He comes into my office, smirking at Erika. "How many emails did you have this morning?" I ask, and he looks at me confused. "Just answer the question."

He puts his hands in his pockets and looks over at Erika, who just smiles. "I don't know. Maybe ten."

"I had four," I say. "Do you think something is wrong with the server?"

"What time did you go home last night?" he asks, and I just look at him. "Just answer the question."

"A little after seven," I say.

"Well, it could be that you answered everything before you left. You don't have to be busy all the time, Becca," he says, and I gasp.

"Don't jinx me. And to answer your question, yes, I have to be busy all the time. It's how I function." He shakes his head and walks out of my office.

"What do you need me to do?" Erika asks. "I can start on a list of things that we need to tackle next month and see if I can get it going now."

"Yes." I point at her, and she smiles and walks out of

my office. I pull out my chair when my phone rings, and my eyes light up. I pick it up and see that it's Nico. My heart speeds up just a bit, and the smile doesn't leave my face. "Well, well, well." I turn in my chair and lean back, looking outside. "To what do I owe the pleasure of this phone call?"

"Well," he says, his voice coming out gruff. "For one, I'm calling to thank you for the care package." When he laughs, I hear the rustling of sheets, and I wonder if he's still in bed. I wonder if he's dating anyone. Oh my God, he's probably dating someone. I'm going over everything in my head, and I'm not liking any of it.

"Well, you are more than welcome," I say, sitting up. My stomach flips and flops at the thought of him with someone else. "I figured the hat was going to a good home."

"That fucking hat," he says, laughing. "You were not joking."

I grab my coffee, taking a sip. "I told you."

"I would have called you yesterday, but something came up." He sounds tired.

"Are you okay?" I ask, and I sit up even straighter. "Is everyone okay? What happened?"

"We had an injury," he says, and my heart sinks. "None of your guys."

"I mean, thank God but …" I shake my head. "How bad?"

"Bad enough I'm calling you for a favor." His voice is soft. "Definitely not the reason I wanted to have to call you," he says, and I wonder what he means by that, "but

I need help."

"I mean, I can try," I say. "What did you have in mind?"

"I need a right-winger," he says, and I look up at the ceiling.

"It's November," I say. "You know that teams are just starting to get into their groove in November."

"There has to be someone somewhere who isn't happy," he says. "Don't tell me you can't do this."

I laugh. "Are you trying to get me fired up?" I ask. It's his turn to chuckle, and I can picture what color his eyes are now.

"I'll do whatever it takes," he says.

"I can reach out to a couple of my guys to see, and we can go from there," I say. "I know of two who would love to get traded but—"

"From where?" he asks, and without telling him who, I name the team. It doesn't really matter because I have at least one client on each team.

"Tampa and Detroit," I say. "Let me make a few calls and then you do the rest. But you have to know that I have no say in any of these. I deal with the contracts, not the trading."

"I know the GM for both those teams, and we are on good terms, so you never know. You just get me the names of the players who are interested in trading, and I'll do the rest from here."

"Okay," I say. "Give me a couple of hours." I disconnect from him and call Graham, who plays for Detroit.

"Hey," he says, answering right away. "What's up?"

"Not much." I play it cool. "You know me, just calling to check in. How is everything?"

"Meh," he says. "My game is stuck at a standstill when I'm playing on the fourth line." He starts to complain, and this is what I need.

"What do you want me to do?" I ask. "I can talk to Martin," I mention the team general manager, "and see what he says."

"I don't want him to get pissed at me and send me down to the farm team," he says, and I shake my head.

"If he wants to send a five-million-dollar player down to the farm team when his team is going on a six-game losing streak …" I laugh. "I'll call you back." I pick up the phone and call Martin, who answers after four rings.

"Hello?" he says, and I almost roll my eyes. I know damn fucking well he has my number stored in his phone. Last year, he wanted one of my players, a free agent, and he called me nonstop for two months.

"Martin"—I tap my nail on the desk—"it's Becca."

"Hey, Becca, what can I do for you?" he asks.

"Well, I'm calling to ask you a couple of things," I say. "I was just talking to Graham, and we were wondering where you think it's going."

He huffs out, and I don't give him a chance to speak. "I'm just asking. He's going to be a free agent at the end of the year, and if you keep him on the fourth line, chances are his numbers are going to go down."

"You telling me how to run my team?" he says with a tone I don't care for. It's the tone all men use for *I have a bigger penis than everyone*. It's also a tone that I know means I'm right.

"I'm just worried about my client," I say. "At the end of the day, I don't care if you play your goalie as a forward." I sit up. "I care that if you aren't going to play him, then why don't we look at getting him on another team, and you can both be winner?"

"What the fuck does that mean?" he says.

"Martin, his contract is for five million a year," I say, something he already knows. "When he becomes a free agent, I'm going for more. I mean, that isn't a surprise. His numbers have always been good. He's always been the top scorer even when he was with Pittsburgh." Something else he already knows. "But if you are looking for a fourth-line player, you can get two players for the price of that one contract."

"You have brass balls, Becca," he says, and I smirk, knowing that I have him right where I want him.

"I heard some talk out of Dallas that they would like him," I say, cutting to the chase.

"Have Nico call me," he says. I throw my hands in the air and smirk, but he disconnects before I have a chance to thank him. I couldn't care less how hurt his ego is.

I dial Nico, who answers right away. "It's been less than an hour."

I smile when I hear his voice and ignore all my feelings at the moment. This is business. This is what I'm made for. "Well, what can I say? I'm good at what I do."

"What do you have for me?" he asks.

"Graham Burns," I say. "His contract is five million. He's a free agent at the end of the year. His numbers are good, not great because he's playing the fourth line," I say what I told Martin. "I'm going for more when his contract expires."

"Well, thanks for the heads-up," he says. "I know of him. I'll give Martin a call."

"I might have suggested that he can get two players for one of Graham," I say. "Just in case."

"I'll let you know," he says, and I call Graham back.

"Hey," I say when he answers the phone. "I wanted to give you a heads-up that Nico is going to talk to Martin about you."

"Dallas," he says, and then I hear his voice go low. "They are doing okay except for last night they got killed in Buffalo."

"Yeah, well, we all have off games," I say. My other line rings, and I see it's Nico.

"I'll call you back," I say. "But I think it's safe to say you should pack your bags," I say, going to the other line. "Hello?"

"He's mine. I'm going to get him," he says. "I'm in New York, so I'm going to hop over to Detroit."

"What are the terms?" I ask.

"I'm buying the contract from him," he says. "His cap space is at the top, and he can bring up some players from the farm team."

"Then I guess we both win," I say, and he laughs.

"I owe you, Becca," he says, and his voice goes soft. "And it's going to be a debt I want to pay off. I'll call you when I'm back in town." He hangs up without giving me a chance to say anything. I don't even know what I would have said. He stunned me with the way his voice went soft when he said my name, and then dropped to almost a whisper.

I put my phone down on the desk, and my eyes don't move from it. It buzzes, and I look down to see it's from Graham.

Graham: I'm coming to Dallas. He promised me second line.

Me: Once he sees how you play, he'll bump you up to the first line.

Graham: Fingers crossed. I'll see you soon. I play New York tomorrow.

Me: I'll be watching.

He sends me back a smiling emoji. My phone beeps again, and this time when I look down, my eyes blink more times than needed.

Nico: Keep Saturday free.

EIGHT

NICO

MANNING: MEETING AT six. Hope you can make it.

Me: Send me the address, and I'll be there.

The last text is from one of my oldest friends, Laurene. The two of us both come from wealthy families, so we would always hang out at forced gatherings.

Laurene: Hey, long time, no talk. Give me a shout.

I put my phone down and call for Lizzie. "You rang," she says, coming into my home office. I look up at her. "If you called me in here to make you coffee, I'm going to …" We got home this morning and just decided to head home.

I put up my hand to stop her from telling me what she would do to said coffee. I learned a long time ago that she was my assistant, but she would never fetch me coffee. To prove her point, she would get the order wrong every time, or she served it scalding with no milk. It was just not going to happen. "I have a meeting at six."

"Do I have to come?" she asks, and I shake my head. "Is it Manning?"

"Yes," I say. Manning came over not too long ago to let me know that he's leaving his wife. I wasn't shocked in the least, and it was about time. I've worked with Murielle a couple of times, and all I wondered was how someone like Manning could be with her. She wasn't horrible per se, but she wasn't the nicest. Where Manning does not want to be recognized, she wants everyone to know what she is doing.

"I mean, I'm not going to say it's about time," Lizzie says, "but it's about fucking time. That woman is horrible." I look at her, pinching my eyebrows together. "I didn't tell you, but once in the beginning, she thought I was going after Manning because I laughed at his joke. Called me a horny bitch and told me to stay away from her man."

I look at her in shock. "Why didn't you tell me?"

"Because it was a non-issue," she says, and I just shake my head. "Are you going to let her keep her position on the foundation?"

"As long as she acts respectfully, I don't see why not," I say, and she laughs.

"That lady wouldn't know respect if it came to the house and knocked on her door," Lizzie says. "I also have the press release ready for Manning."

"Perfect, I'll let you know when to release it," I say, and she gets up. "You can take the rest of the day off," I say, and she throws her head back and laughs.

"So kind of you," she says. "It's four thirty."

I laugh, looking at my Rolex. "Okay, then take tomorrow off."

"Bye," she says, walking out and holding her hand up in a wave. "See you tomorrow."

She is not one to just lay around and take the day off, even if I suggest she should. I get up and go to my bedroom to slip on something more comfortable. The past three days have been a fucking roller-coaster ride.

From rushing to Buffalo to signing Graham, it's just one thing after another. I smile, thinking about how none of it would have been possible without Becca. I don't know what she told Martin, but he didn't even try to fight to keep Graham.

After changing into my jeans, I grab a white T-shirt and slip it on. Grabbing my keys and leather jacket, I walk out of the house and make my way over to the address Manning sent me. I pull up and see the lights on inside and outside.

I walk up and ring the doorbell, my heart beating a little bit faster than it was before. I blame it on walking to the door, but my head laughs at me. The door opens, and I see Becca. God, she is even more beautiful than she was the last time I saw her. She is wearing white pants that hug her hips but fall to the floor, and her orange turtleneck looks so soft my hands itch to reach out and touch it. To touch her. "Hey," I say to Manning, and then I turn to Becca. "Good to see you."

She just nods at me as the doorbell rings again. I move to the side so she can open the door, and I hold my breath at her proximity and tuck my hands in my pockets to stop from touching her. Candace comes in, and I wonder how she is doing with all this.

I follow everyone into the dining room, listening to Becca talk, and I'm not surprised about what all she did. I just lean back in my chair and watch how she handles herself. The way she taps her finger on the table when she's listening.

"Hopefully, this will be over very soon, and we can pop champagne for another reason," I say, getting up at the end of the conversation after Jaxon calls his father. "Becca, why don't I take you to dinner?" The words are out of my mouth before I can take them back, and I look at her, afraid that if I look at Manning and Candace, they will see something I don't want anyone to see right now.

Becca looks at me and tilts her head to the side. "Depends on what you're thinking." I can even see the little smile she tries to hide.

"Whatever you want." *Game on.* She stands and closes her laptop.

"I'm thinking pizza," she says, "in Italy."

I look at my watch and do the calculations in my head. "If we leave now, we can get there for lunch." She turns, and we say goodbye to everyone, and I walk out with her.

"So where are we going?" she asks, standing beside her SUV. I want to wrap my hand around her waist and pull her to me. Lean down and kiss her lips. *Fuck, this is not good.*

"Why don't I follow you to your house? You can drop

off your car, and then we can decide," I say, opening her door for her without giving her a chance to think about anything. She gets in, but I can see her mind spinning. "Relax, Becca."

"I'm usually the one in charge," she says.

I lean in with one hand on the door and the other hand on top of the SUV. "When it's you and me, I'm the one in charge," I say, and I see her eyes go a deeper green. I could easily lean in just a touch more and find out what she tastes like, but instead, I step back and close the door.

I walk to my SUV and make plans while I follow her back to her place. She hands her keys to the doorman and walks over to my SUV. I get out and open the door for her. "Thank you," she says, getting in the SUV. I get in and look over at her as she puts her seat belt on.

"It's killing you, isn't it?" I ask, and she rolls her lips and nods her head.

"You have no idea," she says and turns to me. "Are you going to give me a hint?"

"Okay," I say, pulling away from her building. "Originally, I was going to fly us to New York." She gasps in shock.

"I was kidding about having pizza in Italy," she says. "Okay, fine, I wasn't but New York?"

"Yeah, if it was earlier, we could have done it, but it's almost seven, so we wouldn't get there until ten, which is eleven with the time change."

"You're serious?" She turns and puts her back to the door. "You were going to take me to New York at the drop of a hat."

"Yeah," I say. "I figured I owed you a lot more than that." I look over at her, and I wonder if I kiss the shit out of her would her lips still shine like they do now. Putting the SUV in the park, I look over at her. "Until I can do more, this will have to do," I say, reaching for the door and opening it. I walk around the SUV, seeing her leg come out. Her red bottom shoes suddenly make me think of sex. It's all fucking Lizzie's fault. She stands and turns to shut the door. I can't even tell if she's wearing underwear under those white pants.

"Where are we?" she asks, looking around.

"This might not be Italy," I say, grabbing her hand. Our fingers intertwine with ease. Neither of us says anything else as we look down at our hands locked together.

The restaurant lights shine, and I look around and don't see any empty tables outside for us to eat at. I open the door to the restaurant with my free hand and hold it open for her to walk through with me following. Her hand remains in mine like neither of us wants to let go.

"For two, please," she tells the hostess, who looks at me and then back at her. We follow the hostess through the crowded restaurant to a table in front of the big red wood-burning oven.

Slipping my hand out of hers, I pull out a chair for her. She sets her purse in the chair next to hers before she sits down. I shrug out of my jacket, and I see her looking over at me. "It's casual day," I say, tossing my jacket on the chair beside me. Instead of sitting in front of her, I decided to sit beside her.

"I've never seen you in anything but a suit," she says

to me as the waitress comes over and hands us the menus. Becca smiles at the waitress and orders herself a white wine and looks over at me.

"A bottle of San Pellegrino," I say, and she nods, walking away. "I've never seen you dressed casually."

She looks up from the menu. "Hello." She points at herself. "This is casual."

"You're wearing heels," I point out.

"I was watching Jaxon all day long," she says, and I look at her, shocked. "Manning needed someone to watch Jaxon while he ran all his errands."

"Wait, I don't understand," I say, putting my menu down and looking at her. "What was your role in all of this?"

She sets her menu down, smiling at the waitress who brings her glass of wine. "We'll need a minute," Becca tells her, and she nods her head, walking away. She takes a sip of wine, tucking her hair behind her ear. "Manning is my client," she tells me, looking down at her fingers as she plays with the stem of the wineglass, "but he's also my friend." I don't interrupt her. "So I did what I needed to do in order to protect him."

"Which means what exactly?" It's me tapping my finger on the table this time as I wait for her to answer.

"I was the one who hired the private investigator. I was the one who got him the house. I was the one who got his mother here."

"You were the one who did all that?" I look at her, shocked, but I don't know why I am. "Is there anything you can't do?"

"Yes," she says, smirking. She picks up her glass of wine and takes another sip. "I can't give up control."

I laugh, and right before I'm about to say something, she shocks me even more. "I don't know why," she says, setting the glass back down, "but for you, I might try."

NINE

BECCA

THE ELEVATOR PINGS, and I step out, smiling. "Good morning," I tell the receptionist, who smiles at me as she answers the phone. I wait for her to put the phone down. "The phone has been ringing off the hook for you."

I smile even bigger. "God, I love those words. Music to my ears," I say and walk back to my office to the sound of my heels clicking on the floor.

"Good morning," I say to Erika, who gets up from her desk and follows me into my office. I slip off my jacket, draping it over the back of my chair. "How is everything?" I ask, sitting.

"You have twenty-five calls about Manning today," she says, and I knew it was coming. When the bomb got dropped last night, I knew the kickback would be today. "I have them all here." She hands me the stack of papers. "By priority, but you can go through it just to make sure.

Is there anything else you need from me?"

I look up at her. "No, thank you, this is great," I say, going through all the papers. She turns and walks out of my office, and my phone rings. I look down to see it's Manning.

"Hello," I say, leaning back in my chair. "If you're calling to ask me for another favor, you are out of luck for the month." He laughs. "I'm not kidding, Manning."

"Actually, I'm calling to thank you," he says.

"I'm afraid to ask you for what?" I try to joke with him.

"For fucking everything. From renting this house to getting my mother here." He lets out a huge breath.

"Your mother was on the next flight out. I didn't even have to guilt-trip her into coming," I say. "She was at the house the next day."

His voice goes low. "I don't know what I would have done without you."

"Well, it's a good thing you pay me well," I joke with him.

"That's bullshit, and you know it," he says. "You might be all cheetah-like, but deep down, you have a soft heart."

"If you let anyone hear you say that—" I say, and he stops me.

"Relax, I'm all alone," he says. "I woke up this morning feeling so free."

"Well, enjoy it because you have a game tonight, and the press is going to be all over you. I'll be there tonight." I wasn't going to go to the game, but I thought it would be a good idea in case he needed me. *You just want to see Nico.*

"Well, considering I don't talk about my private life, it's going to be easy," he says. "Also, you and Candace already put out a statement."

"And judging from the messages on my desk, we've only scratched the surface," I say.

"How bad?" he asks. After all this time, he will forever be the only client of mine who shies away from the press. Even to give interviews, he has to be forced into it.

"*People* magazine wants to do an exclusive," I say, and he laughs. "So does *GQ*, and I think I saw *Hockey News* also."

"Negative on all fronts," he says. "But I do have something that I would like you to do."

I slap my desk. "I knew it," I say. "I knew you needed another favor. Your favor card is all used up."

"It's not a favor," he reassures me. "I want you to meet Evelyn," he says of the woman who finally gave him the strength to stand up to Murielle. "Obviously, whenever it works for you."

"I would love to meet her," I say, and I look up at the door to see Francis standing there with a huge vase of pink roses. "Just tell me when, and I'll clear my schedule," I say, and we hang up. "What is all that?" I ask Francis, who is joined by Trevor, who carries another vase of white roses in his hands.

"We should be asking you that question," he says, putting down the vase in the middle of my desk. "Not one but two," he says, and I look at them in shock as I grab the first little white envelope.

"I haven't the faintest idea," I say, taking out the small white card and reading it.

Becca,

I owe you Italy.

Maybe one day.

Nico

I smile and grab the other envelope. The smile hurts my cheeks, but I can't help it. My hands are shaking as I pull out the other card.

Becca,

Let go.

I'll catch you.

N

I have to sit down after I read the last one. Looking up at my brothers, I say, "Can I just have one second to just …" I can't even right now. My heart is pounding so hard I have to put my hand on my chest.

I force myself to get up and walk to the bathroom off of my office. Closing the door, I'm hit with flashbacks from last night. I spent all night reliving it in my dreams, and it's coming back again.

"I can't give up control," I told him, ignoring all the screaming going on in my head. "I don't know why." I took another sip of wine. "But for you, I might try."

He looked at me, his eyes turning a light blue, and I swear if he looked at me like that all the time, I might do whatever he wants me to. "I'll catch you," he told me, and then the waitress came by, and for the rest of the meal, we tiptoed around whatever that moment was.

We both wanted to talk about what just happened, but we were afraid to have the words out there in the universe. He paid the bill, and when we walked out, our hands grazed each other's. He didn't reach for my hand, and it bothered me. I could have grabbed his, but I was hanging on by a string. I had never been in this type of situation, and I had no idea what the rules of the game were. I don't think he knew, either.

When he pulled up to my building, I looked over at him, taking off my seat belt. "Thank you, Nico," I said and then smirked. "It's no Italy, but it was almost like I was there."

He laughed, and I thought he was going to lean over and kiss me. I had hoped he would, but instead, he just looked at me. "One day, Becca," he said, and before I could even say anything, the doorman had opened the door. I walked into my building without looking back. But I felt eyes on me, and when I stood in front of the elevator doors, I saw him from the corner of my eyes. He was standing next to his SUV as he watched me. I turned for just a second before stepping onto the elevator, and it was the last thing I saw.

"We're still here." I hear Francis say, and I shake my head, looking at myself in the mirror, my cheeks just a touch flushed. I wet my hand with cold water and place my palms on them to cool down. I take one more look at myself before unlocking the door.

I walk out with my head held high and my shoulders back. "What is with you two?" I say, trying to avoid their eyes. "Don't you have work to do?" I don't want them to see how affected I was by the flowers. I put on my poker face right before I turn to them.

"Oh, trust me, I have work to do," Trevor says to me, "but this is a little bit …" He holds his hands out as he thinks of what to say.

"More entertaining," Francis says, going to one of my empty chairs in front of my desk and sitting down. "So …"

"So, what?" I say, sitting down. I pick up the notes in front of me and put them in my top drawer. Then I get back up and smell the flowers. Grabbing one vase, I walk over to the table in the corner and put it in the middle. "I helped a friend."

"You helped a friend, and he sends you fifty roses?" Francis tilts his head to the side, and from his tone, it's more like *yeah, right.*

"Is this who I think it is?" Trevor asks. He's always the one who does the thinking between the two of them. Whereas Francis is I'm jumping off the roof, Trevor is going to list the reasons he shouldn't. Even though Francis is older, Trevor usually has the better sense.

"I did a favor for Nico, and well, he thanked me by sending me flowers."

It's not exactly a lie.

"Nico … Nico …" Trevor asks, saying his name twice, and I roll my eyes. "The Nico who owns the Dallas Oilers?"

"There isn't another Nico we both know." I cross my legs, putting my shoulders back, making me sit up straight. "I don't understand all the questions."

"It's a bad fucking idea," Trevor says, and I look over at him.

"What exactly is a bad idea?" I'm annoyed because I'm not ready to have this conversation with anyone. It's enough that my head is telling me what a bad idea this is. I don't need to hear it out loud.

"You and Nico," Trevor says, and I look at Francis to see what he has to say, but all he does is look over at Trevor. "It's the worst idea you've ever had."

"Nothing is going on." I put my hands up. "He needed a player, and I helped him acquire one. It was a win-win for everyone." They both just stare at me. "And then we had the whole Manning situation and …"

"And we have a policy," Francis says. "The don't shit where you eat policy."

"I am not shitting nor eating anywhere." I point at him. "And you are not exactly the person who should be telling me the rules. You were having an affair with your client's wife."

"Girlfriend," he corrects me. "At the time, she was his girlfriend, and they were on a break. Then they got back together and got married."

"They were on a break." I roll my eyes. "Please."

"Listen, we know that you would never do anything to jeopardize what you have achieved." I swear Trevor's an old soul. "You are also old enough to know what is right and what is wrong."

"Nice talk, Dad," Francis says, getting up. "What dip-shit is trying to say is it's a bad fucking idea," he says, and I think he's done, but he isn't. "A horrible, horrible idea." He turns and walks out of the office.

Trevor gets up. "We'll support you with whatever," he says, walking out of the room, and what was a happy moment turned into so much more doubt than I care to think about. So I don't. Instead, I bury myself in my work, returning phone calls and making sure that all of Manning's sponsors hear from me.

"Are you ready?" Francis says, coming into my office, and I stand to grab my jacket. "Are you not going to change into something more comfortable?"

"No," I say, looking down at my outfit. I'm wearing a fitted one-piece white turtleneck long-sleeved dress with a beige jacket over it. "It's a hockey game."

"And I'm going for work," I say, and he shakes his head.

I walk out with him, and we park in our usual spots, walking into the arena. The phone goes off in my hand, and just as soon as I see who it is, I hear him say my name.

"Becca." I turn my head, and there he is, the man who has slowly crept into my head.

"Nico." I say his name, and it's almost in a whisper.

TEN

Nico

"THE PRESS IS all over the place," I say to Lizzie while we walk the halls of the arena. The fans have started coming in, and I look down, and then it's almost as if my body knows she's close. I look up and around, and I spot her right away. How could I fucking not?

She looks like sex on a fucking stick. My cock becomes semi-hard just looking at her tight ass from the back. My eyes roam all the way down to her fucking sky-high red bottom heels. Lizzie was right—those shoes scream sex. I've never actually noticed fucking shoes before, but with her wearing them, the only thing I can think of is fucking her while she wears them.

"Is that Becca?" I hear Lizzie from beside me. "Only she could pull off that look at a game."

"Becca." I call her name as soon as I get close to her, and when she turns, I swear I feel like someone kicked me in the stomach. Not only is her hair perfectly styled but the white dress hugs her every fucking curve. The front of her shoes are white, and the back has a leopard print. But what gets me the most is her red-painted lips that scream to be kissed.

"Nico," she says my name in a whisper, and if I wasn't closer, I wouldn't have heard her.

"I didn't know you were coming to the game," I say once I stand in front of her.

"I thought Manning could use the support," she says and then looks over at Lizzie. "You look amazing," she tells her, and Lizzie laughs.

"I'm in awe every single time I see you," Lizzie says, and then the guy next to Becca sticks out his hand.

"Hi," he says, and Lizzie turns to him. "I'm Francis, Becca's brother." I look at him, and not one part of him resembles her.

I see Lizzie look at his hand, and she reluctantly shakes it. "Lizzie. I'm Nico's right-hand."

I'm watching the exchange between Francis and Lizzie when I hear Becca laugh. "From what I've seen, she's your right and half your left."

I look over at Lizzie, who nods her head in agreement. "Sometimes I'm both arms."

"Do you guys have seats?" I ask, and I see Lizzie shaking her head.

"They own the box next to yours," she whispers in my ear, and I laugh.

"Forgive me," I say. "I'm usually in the press box and not in my actual box."

"Well, I don't know about you guys," Francis says,

"but I could use some food and a drink. Lizzie, would you care to join me?"

"I'm working," she says to him, "but I think those four girls whispering behind you might be available." Lizzie looks at me. "If you need me, text me." She looks at Becca. "I'll see you soon." Then she turns back to Francis, who stands there with his hands in his pockets. "Francis, nice meeting you."

He smirks at her. "The pleasure was mine." He's about to say something else when she walks away from him, leaving him hanging.

"She's a smart girl," Becca says to Francis, and he just shakes his head.

"I'll meet you in the box," he says and nods, walking away from her.

"How are things?" I ask, and she looks down at the floor and then up.

"I got the flowers," she says. "Sorry I didn't text you. It's been a crazy day."

"How many calls came in for Manning?" I ask. I had over one hundred calls, so I could just imagine how many she had.

"Serious ones?" She looks at me. "About fifty. Then about five hundred bullshit ones."

"How did you know which were serious and which weren't?" I ask, and someone walks by her, hitting her shoulder. I reach out my hand and hold her arm. "We should get out of the way." My hand falls from hers, and I want to grab hers as we walk away from the crowd and toward the stairs that lead to the private boxes. Instead, we walk with our hands beside each other. I notice the men do a double-take when they look over at her. I've been around beautiful women before, and most times, they know the looks they are going to get but not Becca. She walks like she's on the catwalk and doesn't even notice the men and even some women looking at her. Instead, she walks with the confidence of a woman who knows what she wants.

"Have dinner with me." I look over at her as we walk up the stairs. "Not here. After the game."

"I don't think that's a good idea," she says when we get to the top of the steps, and I see two reporters approaching us.

"Nico," one of them says.

"Christopher." I say his name, and then he looks at Becca.

"If it isn't the super agent," he says, and Becca laughs.

"I don't know about super agent," she says, "but I did have my cape dry-cleaned." Even I laugh.

"So what's it going to be?" he asks her, and she tilts her head to the side. "Manning."

"Mr. Simmons," she says, using his last name, and I know from her tone that this is the business Becca. "You know full well my client doesn't give interviews."

"There are so many rumors," he says, and she just rolls her eyes.

"You know the saying, those who feed on rumors are small suspicious souls." His eyes almost bug out of his head. "Now that isn't you, Mr. Simmons, is it?" Before he can even answer, she gives him more to stew on.

"Weren't you the one who spilled the beans on someone's wife being pregnant even before they told their families?"

"That was an accident," he says with his teeth clenched. "I apologized."

"Oh, I heard," she says. "Now, I would hate for you to get stuck in another snafu because of a rumor." The sound of clapping fills the arena. "Oh, that's my cue," she says, smiling at him. "Have a great evening, Christopher." She turns and walks away from him, going straight to her owner's box.

"That woman," he says under her breath, and I just glare at him.

"I suggest that you keep whatever comment you were going to make right then to yourself," I say, and he just looks at me. "Besides, the way I just saw it, she handed you your balls on a platter."

"Whatever," he says and walks away from me. The other reporters just laugh.

"He never learns." He shakes his head, and I walk to the box where she just entered. Opening the door, I find the box empty, but I see her jacket on the couch next to her purse.

Every single box is almost the same. A living room area in the back with a bar right against the edge where you walk down and have ten seats. Looking around the box, I see the logo of her firm on the walls and pictures of her with the clients that she has.

The television on the wall has the view from the ice. The bathroom door opens, and when she steps out and I see her without the jacket, my first thought is the dress needs to be burned and never worn again. It's showing you her whole body, but it keeps you guessing. Or at least it keeps me guessing. I wonder what bra she is wearing under the outfit. "Oh, hey," she says when she sees me walking over to the bar and taking a bottle of white wine out of the fridge. "Sorry about just walking away, but that fucking man gets under my skin."

"Well, if you're keeping score. It's Becca one, Christopher zero," I say, looking around. "Where is everybody?"

"I don't know who this everybody is you're referring to?" She takes her glass of wine and takes a sip.

"The box is empty," I say, looking around. "You get twenty-five tickets with each box."

"Yeah and?" she says, walking toward me. "We give out Saturday games mostly. The week is just mostly us, depending."

"Depending on?" I ask, and she sets the wine down on the table.

"Depending on if any of my other clients are coming into town. I usually meet with them for lunch or dinner the day before if time permits it."

"Who do you root for?" I ask. Reaching out my hands, I hold her hips and pull her a bit closer to me. I can smell her citrus perfume. It smells like fresh lemons and sunshine.

"That depends," she says, her own hands holding the lapels of my blue jacket. "I usually just root for whoever wins." She steps closer, and even with her heels, she still has to tilt her head back in order to look up at me.

"Wrong answer, Becca," I say softly, and she chuckles.

"Why is that?" she asks. "For me, I win either way."

"I hate to lose," I say, and I'm not talking about hockey anymore. I don't know what it is about her, but she's making me go crazy, and she has no fucking clue either.

"No one likes to lose, Nico," she says. All I can think about is her saying my name over and over again while I bury myself inside her.

"You've gotten under my skin, Becca," I say.

"I thought nothing gets under your skin." She smirks and moves in closer, placing her palms flat on my chest.

"I thought so, too, and then …" I bend my head down ever so slowly. "Then there was you," I say as my lips get closer to her. "You know what I thought when I saw you today?" I murmur. "I thought that your lips were made for me to fucking kiss."

"Nico," she says with a sigh, and it's the last thing she says before my lips are on hers. Her mouth opens for mine, and when my tongue slips into her mouth, I swear the world stops. Her tongue slides against mine, and my hands move up to her face. Our heads move from one side to the other, both of us fighting against the other. Her hands finally move from my chest upward as her chest presses against mine. She wraps her arms around my neck, and we both moan.

The sound of talking gets closer, causing us to move away from each other. "No chance in hell." We both hear Francis from the hallway.

We don't have a chance to say anything else before the door opens, and he comes in, followed by the four girls hanging around him downstairs. "Hey, you two."

I nod at him and put my hands in my pockets to hide the fact my cock is hard as a rock. I look at her, and if my cock wasn't hard before, it definitely would have gotten hard looking back at her. Her eyes are an emerald color, and the tint of pink trails down to her chest. But it's her lips that make me get even harder. They are plumper than before and are still painted the brightest red.

ELEVEN

BECCA

"BECCA." HEARING MY name, I look up from my phone toward Matthew Grant.

I smile at him, getting up from my chair. "Mr. Grant," I say, holding out my hand, and he just shakes his head.

"Enough with the Mr. Grant bullshit," he says. "It's Matthew." I laugh at him. "Follow me," he says, and I take my cashmere jacket and my wine-colored Louis Vuitton bag that matches my shoes and sweater. "Is it cold enough for you?" he asks, seeing me put my jacket over my arm.

"I love New York," I say, "from April to October." He laughs as he holds open the glass door to the conference room.

The big brown table in the middle has black leather seats all around it. Water bottles sit in the middle of the table, and the New York Stingers logo paints the wall. Pictures of them with the Cup throughout the years hang all along the wall. "Those are the same months I hate Dallas," he says, pulling out a chair for himself to sit down. I put my jacket and purse in the chair beside him and sit down facing him. "The humidity is enough to make you crazy."

"Fair enough," I say. "Thank you, by the way." I sit down in the chair. "I hated to cancel our meeting, but I was needed in Dallas."

He nods his head. "I got to give you that." He looks at me. "You handled that like no one else," he says of Manning and the fucking blowup I handled.

"Between you and me," I say, "it's always easy when you have someone who won't run his mouth." Matthew puts his hands on the table.

"You've got that fucking right," he says. "MC is on his way up," he says, and I look at him. "That is Cooper's nickname. With my father and the other kids, it was always MC even when he was younger, and it stuck with him."

When the glass doors open, I look up to see Cooper come in, and he is the stamp of his father, just a touch skinnier. He wears track pants and a black T-shirt. His baseball cap sits backward, and you see the hair coming out in the back. I get up. "Cooper," I say, putting out my hand. "Becca."

"Nice to meet you," he says. After shaking my hand, he walks to his father and gives him a hug.

"Did you eat?" Matthew asks him, and he looks just a touch embarrassed.

"Dad," he says, "I'm almost eighteen."

"You could be almost a hundred, and I'd still ask you," Matthew says, sitting down. "Now answer my question."

"I had a protein shake. I was going to grab something, but I was running late," Cooper says, looking at the water bottles and grabbing one. "I didn't want to be late." He looks at me, and I smile.

Matthew looks at me. "Did you eat?" he asks, and I nod.

"Please order the man some food," I say, and Cooper groans while Matthew picks up the phone and calls an order in.

"Sorry about that," he says, sitting down.

"It's fine. We can talk until the food gets here," I say, and Cooper looks at me. "I'm sure you're wondering why I wanted to sit down with you." I don't make him answer. "I mean, getting drafted, there is nothing I can do for you." I look at Matthew. "There is nothing that anyone can do. I can't negotiate even the starting salary." I look at Cooper. "But I'm not just thinking about Cooper, the hockey player. Who is Cooper Grant?" He looks at me, not sure what I mean. "What does Cooper Grant stand for?"

He sits up, playing with the water bottle in his hand. "Hockey."

I nod at him. "Family." I tap my nail on the table when he looks at Matthew, who just looks at me smirking.

"Let me tell you what I see when I look at Cooper Grant," I say.

"Oh, this is going to be good," Matthew says.

"I see the top rookie of the year." He smiles, his eyes

lighting up. "With that comes sponsorships from two, maybe even three sports companies." Cooper's eyes light up. "I see the Cooper who works out in the gym. Tracksuit, shirts, shorts." Cooper looks at his father. "You are talking about sponsorship for even nutrition products."

"What about hockey camps and schools?" he asks.

"The sky is the limit," I say. "The question is, how much do you want it?"

"Fuck, Becca," Matthew says, and I look at him. "I've told him that since he was young."

"Look, I can't promise you that it'll come in six months or one year," I say. "Let's be real. When you're drafted, it's to a team at the bottom of the barrel. Usually, the team is rebuilding. You aren't going to be starting with the Stanley Cup champions."

"That is what I told him," Matthew says. "It's going to be rough."

"You are going to be with a team that will probably be shit on day in and day out. It's going to be a learning curve, especially for you since you're at the top of the league right now. It's like when you graduate from middle school. You are the cool kid at the back of the bus, and then you start high school, and you're in the front of the bus again while the cool kids sit in the back. We all know that sucks. But what I can promise you is that I'm going to work as hard as you do. I'm going to get those meetings for you." I lean back in the chair. "Your father knows I have the contacts. He also knows how I work."

"She's good," he says to Cooper, who looks over at him.

"But," I say, "if you sign with me." I look at both of them. "I only give you two passes."

"What does that mean?" Cooper asks, sitting back.

"It means you can fuck up twice," I say. "You shouldn't fuck up at all. But you're young, and well …"

"She's talking about the girls," Matthew says.

"Not just the girls. The partying, the travel, the fame. NHL is another level. It's like a rock star going from playing small venues to selling out stadiums. Shit will be thrown at you." The kid is going to be thrown in the lion's den no matter what family they come from. It's like taking a kid to Disney for the first time. The lights, the people, the attractions. You want to run in every single direction.

"Shit you should stay away from," Matthew cuts in. "Don't follow in my shoes." I don't know the full details of what happened, but he came out swinging and slowly dwindled.

"You get two passes, and on the third one, I walk away," I say.

"Just like that?" he asks, shocked at my bluntness.

"Just like that." I sit up, putting my hands on the table. "I can't stand by if you aren't going to be the one fighting for you."

"I want to be the best," he finally says. "I know my grandfather is the leader on every single record. I know so is my dad. But I want to be better. I want to be the one kids want to be like."

"Then let me help you," I say. "It'd be an honor to be by your side."

"I want it," Cooper says, looking at his dad. "What do you think?"

"I'm not going to decide for you, son," Matthew says. "This is all you. You worked hard to be where you are. You did all this on your own." Cooper nods his head. "Now if you're asking my opinion." He looks at me when he talks. "If you want the best, she's the best. There is no mistake about it. You can ask your uncles." I laugh.

"He is on the top of the list," I say of Justin, who is looking for a new agent. I don't tell them that I'm meeting with him tomorrow afternoon, and if that all works out, I'll be signing him and Evan also.

"I've had a chance to work with her. She's made me say not very nice things to her," Matthew admits, and I laugh.

"I'm shocked." I wink at Cooper. "Not really," I whisper. "It makes me feel even better when they go toe-to-toe with me because I usually win." Cooper smiles and looks down. "Listen, no one is going to put pressure on you. Take the night, take the weekend. Talk to your father, your uncles." I start to get up. "Listen to your gut, Cooper." He nods at me. "Your father has my number."

Matthew nods at me a silent thank you for not beating down his throat for an answer. I grab my jacket and put it on. "I'm here until Sunday." I grab my purse.

"Let me walk you out," Matthew says, leading me down the hallway.

"Thank you," he says quietly, and I look at him. "For telling him the truth." I just look at him.

"I'm not going to name names, but I met with someone today, and they promised him he would be the next big thing. They almost said that they are going to deliver him leprechauns and glitter farts." I laugh as we stop in front of the elevators, and I press the button to go down. "But you told him that he's going to go to the last-place team, and it'll be a while before he ever wins a Cup."

"Reality," I say. "Think about it. Six hundred and ninety players are in the NHL, and only twenty-three players win a ring every year. Some of the best players in the league never win a Cup," I say, and he knows.

The ping of the elevator makes me look up, and I come face-to-face with Nico. His face as shocked as mine as he steps out of the elevator. "Fancy meeting you here," he says, looking at me. His smile forms on his lips, and my stomach does a flip and then sinks. My mouth becomes dry while my palms sweat. My heart starts to beat so fast it echoes in my ears.

Last night, we shared our first kiss—the most amazing kiss I've ever had in my life. He left the box a minute after Francis appeared with the girls. I wanted to throat punch my brother for interrupting us, but instead, I pretended to watch the game. I can't even tell you if anyone scored during the game.

I stayed until the second period and then snuck out without telling him anything. I wasn't ready to talk about it. I'm still not ready to talk about it. I thought I would have the weekend to run through it in my head. I was even staying two days longer than I needed to, just to keep from being tempted to pick up the phone and call him.

"I was meeting with Cooper Grant," I say and hold my arm out to stop the elevator doors from closing and leaving me in this awkward place. "My car is waiting," I lie through my teeth, and I can swear his eyes narrow a bit, calling me out on the lie. "Matthew, thank you so much for taking the time to sit with me."

"Thank you, Becca, for everything," he says, and I smile at them both and walk into the elevator.

"See you soon, Becca," Nico says, and I'm not sure if he's asking me or telling me. His eyes stare straight into mine as the elevator doors close.

TWELVE

Nico

"SEE YOU SOON, Becca." I watch the elevator doors close, and everything in me screams to go after her. Instead, I go with my gut and let her get away. For now.

I've been trying to get in touch with her all fucking day. I've called, and it's gone to voice mail. I've sent texts, and it's been radio fucking silence. When I went to find her after the game, the box was dark and empty. I stood there in the exact place where I kissed her for the first time. Anyone could have seen us, but I didn't give a shit, which is very unlike me. I don't give anyone anything when it comes to my private life because it's the only thing that's mine, and no one has a say in it. "Matthew," I say, turning to him. "Thank you for meeting with me."

"Of course," he says, turning around, going toward the conference room. "This is different, isn't it?"

I laugh. "Well, neither of us wants anything from the

other person, so I guess it is very different." I've been in the game long enough to know that you always want Matthew Grant on your side and you don't fuck with him. Matthew was the one who alerted me about Ralph. For that, I will always owe him.

The meeting lasts a whole two hours. Only when I'm in the elevator and pressing the lobby button do I take out my phone and see that she still hasn't called or texted me. The doors open, and I walk across the lobby, calling Lizzie.

"Well, look who it is." She answers the phone, and I stop walking when I hear her giggle. "Were your ears ringing?"

"No, why?" I ask.

"I'm having lunch with Laurene, and she was telling me how she's been texting you, and you haven't replied." She's texted me four times, the last text letting me know she was coming back home from Europe.

"Shit," I say, stepping out into the cold New York afternoon. It's almost five, and the streetlights are already on. "Tell her I'm going to have to take a rain check for dinner." We were planning on meeting for dinner tonight, but then I saw Becca, and all plans were cancelled.

"She says that you better have a good ass reason for blowing her off, and it better not be for another debutant." I laugh because she knows full well that I never dated a debutant. They were interested in one thing and one thing only. Marriage.

"She knows full fucking well I don't date those women," I tell Lizzie, and I hear her moving, so I know she is walking away from the table.

"Are you having dinner with Matthew?" she asks, and I can hear the smile in her voice. The voices and glasses from the restaurant are quiet, so I know she stepped away.

"No. Actually …" I say, and then she shocks me.

"Would you be having dinner with Becca?" she asks. I see the town car drive up to the curb. The driver gets out of the car and comes over, but I open the door myself.

"How do you know Becca is in town?" I ask, closing the door. "The hotel," I say to the driver.

"Well, I saw her coming out of the building when I dropped you off," she says. "So we shared a ride over to her hotel."

"Where is she staying?" I ask, and Lizzie laughs.

"I knew that is why you were canceling with Laurene," she hisses out. "I knew something more was going on there. I knew it, I knew it, I knew it! I should be a private investigator."

"I had no idea she was in town," I answer honestly. "Not for a minute," I tell her.

"Yeah, right." I can see her rolling her eyes.

"I swear to you, Lizzie. I was shocked when I saw her with Matthew. I had no clue." I wait for her to listen to me. "So where is she staying?"

"Are you going to show up at her place like a freaking creepy stalker?" Lizzie says. "Listen, I don't date often, but if someone just showed up at my door, it would send out alarm bells."

"You live in a gated community," I inform her, "with

a twelve-foot wrought-iron gate. If someone did show up, it would definitely set off alarm bells." I laugh at her.

"Touché," she says. "She's staying at our hotel."

"By any chance …" I say, but Lizzie already knows the question I'm going to ask.

"You think she would give me her fucking room number? What is wrong with you?" she asks. "Nico." Her voice goes low. "Listen, I don't think you showing up at her door is a good idea. What if she's with someone?" The minute the words come out of her mouth, a whole bunch of emotions run through me. I feel like someone kicked me in the balls. My stomach suddenly feels like I'm going to be sick. My palms are clammy, but the worse one is the fucking anger I feel. It's almost as if I see black. I can't listen to the words Lizzie is saying because I hear nothing. The sound in my ears is ringing as we pull up to the hotel.

"I have to go," I say and walk into the private door. "I'm looking for someone who is staying here," I tell the doorman who just listens to me. "Becca." I don't even have to say her last name for me to know that he knows exactly who I'm talking about when his face goes to a sly smirk. The look I give him stops him from making the smirk go to a smile.

"She's staying on the eleventh floor," he says, and I want to laugh since I'm staying on that floor also. "Eleven twenty-two."

"Thank you," I say, getting onto the elevator and pressing the button to the eleventh floor. I walk down the plush carpet to her room and knock on the door. I hear her yell that she's coming.

She opens the door, and I know I'm not the one she's expecting to see standing here. "Nico," she says, her voice almost low. She's dressed in the same outfit she was wearing when I saw her, but with the jacket off, I can get my fill of her. Her beige pencil skirt hugs her hips. The same hips that my hands squeezed twenty-four hours ago. Her long-sleeved sweater is pulled up to her elbows.

"I guess you were expecting someone else?" I ask. Walking into the hotel room, I look around to see if anything indicates she is with someone.

"I was expecting my room service," she says, closing the door and walking over to me. "How did you—"

I cut her off when I grab her face and kiss her lips. Her mouth opens for me to slide my tongue in, and I can taste her sweetness. I thought kissing her last night was a dream. It almost felt too fucking perfect, but with my hands on her face again, this time feels even better than it did last night. Her hands go inside my jacket to my waist, and I can feel her nails digging into me when she pulls me closer to her. I turn my head to the other side as our tongues duel—neither of us giving in.

The knock on the door startles us, making us jump apart. Our chests are rising and falling as if we just sprinted over the finish line of a marathon. She puts her shoulders back and walks to the door, opening it for the room service. The man smiles at her as he pushes in the cart. "Would you like it in the living room?" he asks, and she nods.

"Thank you," Becca says, looking at him and then at me. "I'll pour the tea myself." He smiles at her and walks out.

"Tea?" I ask, smiling.

"It's ginger tea," she says, walking over to the tray. "And it was cold outside."

"Did you order food?" I ask, knowing full well she didn't.

"It was too early to eat. I had a late lunch," she says, pouring herself some tea.

"Have dinner with me," I say, and she looks up. "Unlike yesterday, when you hightailed it out of the arena without seeing me."

She sits back on the couch. "I didn't hightail it anywhere. I was just done for the day."

"So you didn't run off because I kissed you?" I ask, and I have to put my hands in my pockets.

"Let's just get one thing straight. We kissed each other," she says, crossing her arms over her chest.

"I'm the one who kissed you," I say, and when she's about to argue, I put my hand up. "Doesn't fucking matter who kissed who. Bottom line, we kissed, and you ran away."

"I didn't run away." She smirks at me, and I see that her lipstick is still on. "I walked." I just watch the twinkle in her eye. "Fast."

I throw my head back and laugh. "Be ready at seven," I say, turning around and walking out of the room. My hand grabs the door handle.

"What if I had plans?" she asks, and I know that she

doesn't because she's asking.

"Do you?" I look over my shoulder as I open the door.

"I don't make plans on the same day I fly in," she says, and I want to laugh because I do the same. "So …"

"See you in three hours," I say. "Dress casual."

"If I say no?" She tilts her head to the side. I stand here, and I wonder if what I'm going to say next will scare her off. But with that look in her eyes, I can't help it.

"If you say no, then we are just going to have to stay in and eat each other." Her mouth opens. "I, for one, am famished." I look around. "You'd look good lying on that table with my mouth buried between your legs." I point at the table and smirk when I see her cheeks getting just a touch pink. "Fuck it, let's just stay in."

"I'll be ready at seven," she says, and I roll my lips. I'm about to close the door when I hear her call my name. "You might want to save room for dessert." She gets up, walking to the door and grabbing it, pulling it open as my hand slides down. "I know I will," she says before she closes the door in my face, leaving me with my mouth hanging open.

THIRTEEN

BECCA

MY HAND TREMBLES as I tie the belt to my red wraparound dress. I look at myself in the mirror as I put on the red lipstick. I had about thirty minutes to get ready, and I took out the sexiest thing I brought with me. I didn't think I would wear it because it's a bit shorter than I'm used to, but it looks good with the thigh-high black boot stilettos. I turn to check and see how it looks from the back, and the gold heel from the shoe makes it even sexier. The sleeves are also long and flowy, and the silkiness to it makes it even feel sexy.

I make sure everything is in place when I hear a soft knock. "Here goes nothing," I tell myself, turning off the light and grabbing my black purse. I pull open the door, and I know I made the best choice when I see that his mouth is hanging open. "I didn't know where we were going," I say to him.

"Is that a robe?" he asks, and I laugh. "Because it

looks like a robe, and it looks like you shouldn't wear that out."

I throw my head back and laugh. "Well, then I take it you approve." I step out and stand in front of him. "You look good yourself," I say, and to be honest, I haven't even looked at what he's wearing. "But I have to say." I finally look at him and see he's wearing tight black jeans with a charcoal button-down shirt. It's open at the first two buttons, and I reach up, playing with his collar as my nail softly rubs his neck. "I'd prefer if you were naked." I wink at him, and he puts his head back and groans.

"You, Becca," he says, turning and grabbing my hand in his. "You," he says, pushing the elevator call button. "You are going to be the death of me tonight."

"But am I?" I ask as the elevator doors open, and we step in. "Do I need a coat?"

"No," he says, pressing the button, and my heart is beating so fast I don't even care where he takes me. He pulls me to his side, and I look up for a second, and it's just enough time for him to kiss me again. My eyes close as I open my mouth, and he slides his tongue into my mouth. The ping of the elevator makes him leave my lips, and I hear him hissing. "Is that lipstick painted on you permanently?"

I laugh as we walk into the dimly lit room. "You know it's smudge-proof, right?" I whisper in his ear. "I can do a lot of things with this lipstick on like." I turn to look at him when he stops walking. "Drink wine or suck cock," I say as if it's natural to talk about cock in an elegant room like this. I see his eyes glare at me, and his jaw tightens.

"You started this."

"You know what that means, right?" he says to me. "I get to finish it." The way he says that makes a shiver run right through my body

"Good evening," the woman says when she comes back to the hostess table.

"Nico," he says his name. "Suite 1114."

"Right this way, Mr. Harrison," she says, turning and leading us into the restaurant. It's not busy tonight as half the tables are empty. I look up at the crystal chandeliers that are hanging and look so exquisite when they sparkle right over a huge ball of red roses. "Is this table to your liking?" She points at a round table in the back of the restaurant right beside the window.

"It's fine," I say for him when he looks back to see what I think. He pulls out one of the plush velvet gray chairs for me. "Thank you," I say, sitting down in the chair. He sits next to me instead of across from me.

"Good evening," the waiter says when he comes over and pours us glasses of water. "Can I get you a drink to start?"

"I'm going to have a scotch," Nico says, and I look over at him.

"I'm going to have a bottle of wine." He just looks at me. "I don't work tomorrow." He smirks as he looks up at the waiter.

"A bottle of your finest," he says, and the waiter nods at us. "What happened to your two glass max?"

"I figured that this is already a bad idea," I say, putting my hands in front of me. "This whole thing. It's not the best idea." He just looks at me, and I'm dying to know what that face means. I want to ask all the questions, but the waiter comes back with our drinks.

He pours me just a little wine, and the cold white wine slides right down. It's crisp, smooth, and perfect. I nod at the waiter, and he fills my glass. I pick up my glass of wine. "To bad decisions."

He lifts his scotch. "To helping you make those bad decisions." He clicks his glass with mine, and I take another drink.

"Do you want to play a game?" I ask, and he just looks at me. "It's called never have I ever." He rolls his eyes. "So I'm going to say something like never have I ever gotten a lap dance." He looks at me and smirks. "Now, you obviously have so you have to drink."

"How do you know I've gotten a lap dance before?" he asks, and it's my turn to roll my eyes.

"Drink," I say, and he takes a sip of his scotch. "Now it's your turn."

"Never have I ever given a lap dance," he says. I grab my glass of wine, and his eyes glitter. "Are you not going to tell me the story?"

"I mean, I don't know the actual rules to this game," I say. "But I took four years of pole dancing." I clap my hands. "My turn. Never have I ever had sex in public."

I look at him. "Define public."

"I don't know … public. I guess a bathroom in a bar." He doesn't touch his drink. "What do you define as public?"

"No idea, but I've never fucking done it," he says.

"Never have I ever left my house without underwear." I wink at him and take a sip. "Shut up," he says, smiling.

I don't know if it's the easy way this is going or the fact that I've never felt so free before on a date, but I lean in. "Right now," I whisper to him, and his jaw gets tight. "Never have I ever lied about having sex with someone."

He takes his drink, and I throw my head back and laugh. "Please, I'm a guy. Chances are half the stories I told in college that involved a girl were a lie. Never have I ever dated two people at the same time."

I laugh. "Smooth," I say to him. "No, not then. I'm all about one man at a time. And just so we are clear, I also don't stick around if I find out I'm not the only woman." I take my glass of wine and finish it. I look at the ice bucket beside me, and I'm about to grab the bottle and pour myself another glass when the waiter comes rushing over and pours it for me. I take a sip of wine. "Never have I ever said the wrong name during sex." He reaches and drinks his scotch, and I laugh at him. "Oh my God, Nico."

"In my defense, it was Natalia, and I called her Natalie," he says, and I shake my head.

"So if you're inside me, and I call you Nikon, it's the same?" I tilt my head to the side, and he glares at me. "Didn't think so."

"My turn," he says. "Never have I ever had phone sex."

"What?" I say in shock and drink the wine. "I mean, define phone sex."

"You took a drink." He laughs and points out.

I put up my hand. "I mean, I've filtered on the phone sexually before."

"Have you ever had an orgasm on the phone with someone?" he asks, and I look him in the eye.

"Then no," I answer honestly.

"I see lots of firsts in our relationship," he says, and the wine is just flowing through me at this time. I drink the rest of the wine and then look at him. The waiter rushes over, filling my glass, and I just smile at him.

"Never have I ever been shy in the bedroom." My finger taps the stem of the glass, and we both drink at the same time.

"What does that mean, Becca?" he says, and I look at him.

"That means I like sex." I take a drink of wine. "I like having sex. If I want something, I'm not shy about asking for it. Not in the bedroom, not in the kitchen, not in the doorway," I say, and I see that he is fisting his hand. "I like to give." I take a sip of wine and look at the side. "But I like to receive even more." I look at him. "Your turn."

"Never have I ever fell asleep during sex," he says, and I laugh, taking the glass of wine and drinking it.

"It was late and …" I start to laugh. "I didn't really want to, but …"

"Well, one thing is for sure. That isn't going to happen here," he says, and his eyes just look into mine. "Trust me, when we are in bed, no one is going to be falling asleep." I bring the glass to my mouth. "I might fuck you awake, but you'll never fall asleep." He shakes his head.

"My turn. Never have I ever had sex with someone I work with." I don't move my hand, and neither does he. "So we are both in uncharted territory then." I grab my wine for liquid courage and finish the glass. The waiter is there right away to refill it. "We've known each other a long time, Nico," I say. "Why now?"

He takes his drink of scotch, and I have to say he looks just as nervous as I am with asking the questions. "I'm never going to bullshit you," he says, and I lean back in the chair. "I have no fucking idea why now." I lean forward, knowing I need some wine. "I don't know what did it. I can't pinpoint exactly when it happened, but it was like a switch." I know exactly what he means. "I look at you, and it was like what the fuck just happened."

"Like everything was clear now," I say, and he points at me.

"Yes." I look around. "Stay with me," he says. "To-night."

"Where's Lizzie?" I ask, knowing she is also here for work.

"She is staying with a friend," he says. "Besides, she has her own room." I look at him, and I don't know what it is, but with him, I want to jump off the fucking cliff. With the water crashing against the rock, the sounds of thunder coming, I want to jump with him. "So what's it going to be, Becca?" I take the last sip of wine I will for the night. It's more than my two glasses. "Come back to my room with me."

I don't know what the right thing to do is. I have no idea what tomorrow is going to hold. I don't know if I'm going to wake up and regret it. What I do know is that if I don't do it, I'll regret that. I push away from the table. He just looks at me, not sure what is going on. I hold out my hand to him. "Are we going?"

FOURTEEN

Nico

SHE HOLDS OUT her hand for me. "Are we going?" I want to grab her hand and yank her out of there. My cock has been as hard as a rock ever since she told me she isn't wearing anything under that fucking dress.

When she opened the door to her suite, I took one look at her, and the only thing I could focus on was her eyes and the way they lit up. Then I saw her thigh-high boots, and I knew that if she spent the night with me, I'd be fucking her wearing only those fucking boots.

"What are you waiting for?" she asks, tilting her head to the side.

"I want you more than I've wanted anything in a long fucking time," I say, and her hand never moves. "But I'm not going to be going in the category of a bad decision."

"What category do you want to be in?" she asks, and I can see the wheels turning in her head.

"Fuck if I know," I say honestly. "But I do know that I

don't want to be in the category of a bad decision." I lean back in the chair. "I don't think I'm cool enough to hang with the boss hat." Her head goes back, and she laughs.

"You are definitely not as cool as the hat," she says, and her hand falls. I want to jump up from my seat and pick it back up. "How about being in a one-of-a-kind category?" she says, and I just look at her.

"I am one of a kind," I say, standing. "I can totally do that category. But," I say, stepping to her, "I'd rather be in the category of he fucked my brains out all night long." I lean my head in, tilting it to the side. "Do you have that category?"

"I do not," she says, "but I'm excited to start it." I'm the one who laughs as I grab her fingers in mine and walk toward the elevator. "We didn't eat."

I don't answer her until we get into the elevator, and it closes behind me. I turn on her, pushing her into the corner. "I'm going to eat right now," I say to her and squat down in front of her. Her eyes open as I lick her exposed thigh all the way to her uncovered center.

"Nico," she says my name in a breathless whisper right before my tongue slips into her pussy, just as soon as the elevator stops. I'm standing up a second later. "What just happened?" she asks as I pull her to my room.

"I just got into a brand-new category." I wink at her as the door opens. I close it behind her and push her against it.. I don't know why I think she's going to be surprised, but she isn't. Instead, she drops her purse on the floor beside our feet, and her hands are on me. Our mouths crush onto each other. It's all tongue and teeth, both of us fighting to be in charge. My hands are buried in her hair while her hands fight to get my shirt off me. I let go of her mouth and attack her neck. Her leg comes up, hitching over my hip.

"Nico," she says my name, and I look up at her. "Wait." I step away from her. Her hands fall from my chest to the sash tied around her waist. "This would work so much better," she says, pulling on it. The dress opens down the middle, and I see she isn't even wearing a fucking bra. "If I were naked." She shrugs the dress off her shoulders, and it falls by her feet. I take a second to take her in as she stands there in nothing but the fucking heels. Her body is fucking perfect—her hips round, her stomach flat, her tits a perfect fucking handful, and her pussy has a perfect landing strip. My cock goes so hard I think the button of my pants are going to pop off. She walks to me, her hand palming my cock through my pants. "Now this is better," she says as she licks my bottom lip, sliding her tongue inside my mouth for a second and then walking away from me. I turn to watch her; her fucking ass is the best ass I've ever fucking seen. She looks over her shoulder. "I believe someone said they were hungry?"

I follow her as she walks into the big room with a long glossy table with eight chairs. She looks at the table and then the living room area in front of it. "Where do you want to eat?" she asks. I don't answer her because my tongue can't move. I've never been this fucking into someone. In. My. Whole. Life.

She walks over and moves the chair away from the head of the table just a bit. I watch her as she sits on the table right in front of the chair. Her hair falling to the side hides her perfectly shaped dark pink nipples. She slowly opens her legs, letting me see everything she has to offer. She leans back on one hand while one hand slowly moves down to her pussy. She slips a finger inside, and we both moan. I walk to her as she begins to finger fuck herself in front of me. She looks up at me, her hand moving faster and faster. I bend my head and bite her nipple hard. She moans, her finger slipping out of her. I grab her hand, bringing her finger to my mouth, and lick it clean. "Um," she says, looking down at her nipple. My teeth marks appear in in red. "What you do for one, you have to do for the other." She puts her other arm back, and I lean down, taking the other nipple between my teeth. Her hips almost buck up. "Now get to licking." She winks at me.

My hand goes into her hair, and I fist it in my hand, pulling her head back. "What do you want?" I lean over her, and she licks her lips.

"To come," she says. I drop my ass into the seat, and my mouth devours her whole pussy. She goes down on her elbows as she watches me lick up two times before I tease her clit with the tip of my tongue. She moans as I suck it into my mouth, then nibble on it. Her hips move up, so I throw her legs over my shoulders, wrapping my arms around both her legs so she can't move. I suck on her clit again and then circle it with my tongue. Her breathing comes out faster and faster. I open my mouth big and lick from her clit all the way down her slit. I lick up and down slowly and then suck in her clit. Over and over again as slow as I can, knowing she's going to snap.

Her hand goes into my hair, and she tries to get my mouth where she wants it in order to come, but I don't let her. "How do you want to come?" I suck in and then lick up. "I bet you if I put two fingers into you right now, you'd squeeze them."

"Yes," she huffs out, trying to get her hand to her clit so she can play with herself.

"Don't you dare touch it," I say, sitting back in the chair, her pussy dripping wet in front of me. "You touch it, and I'm going to fuck you all night long and not let you come once."

"Why?" she moans. She tries to close her legs, but I stop her. My hand comes out. "Yes." She looks down to see my middle finger slip inside her. "More."

"One more," I say and slip my other finger inside her. "I'm trying to decide," I say as I slowly finger fuck her, stopping when her pussy starts to get tight around my fingers. I slip them out and then lick up once. "How I'm going to fuck you?"

"Any way," she says, wiggling her ass on the table, hoping to get my fingers back. "Fingers."

"I think I'll fuck you on this table first," I say, slipping my fingers into her again as my other hand unsnaps the button to my pants. My cock finally being let loose. "Leg behind your head while I plow into you over and over again."

"Oh my God, yes." She moves her legs up higher, and she holds her ankles beside her head. "Do it."

"Or," I say, taking my fingers out, "bent over." I bite

her clit hard, and I bite her tits, and she starts to shake. "You like that," I say, and she can't talk. Her eyes are half-closed, and she moves her hips side to side. "Bent over the table." I put my two fingers back into her, moving faster. "Holding your tits while I fuck you." My hand goes to my cock, and I moan, and she looks at me.

"Stand up," she says, and I just smirk at her. "I want to see your cock."

"Do you?" I ask as I finger her again, this time curling my fingers up, and her eyes close. "Trust me, by the time the night is over." I flick her clit. "I'm going to fuck that mouth of yours."

"Now," she says, her hands going to her nipples as she pulls them. "Nico, please." I see that her body is shaking with need, so I stand and she sees my cock in my hand. I move my hand up and down, and she licks her lips. "Come in my mouth," she says to me, and I swear to God I would have come right there.

I finger her, and I don't stop when I know she's going to come. Instead, I fuck her faster, and if I didn't care, I would have fucked her with my bare cock. I have to stop thinking about it before all the rules about fucking with a condom go out the window. "I'm coming," she says, and I lean forward, sucking her clit while I finger her. She comes on my hand so much it leaks down to my wrist. When she's done, she sits up, and in two blinks of an eye, she's on her knees, and my cock is hitting the back of her throat. "Fuck," I hiss as she tries to take me all the way down. Her hands move as fast as mine were, and I wish I had time to enjoy it. But I see that she's stroking my cock with one hand and playing with herself with the other one, and I close my eyes. "I'm going to come," I say.

She takes her mouth off me, and I think she is going to make me come on her, but instead, she looks up at me. "Give it to me," she says right before she swallows my cock and works me even faster. My balls tighten, and my hands go to her head as I fuck her face with abandonment. The sound of her gagging doesn't even make me stop. When I come, I throw my head back and call out her name, and she swallows everything that I have.

FIFTEEN

BECCA

"**W**HAT THE FUCK is that noise?" I hear Nico say from beside me. I know it's my phone, but my body can't fucking move. I open one eye and see I'm on my stomach in the middle of the bed or maybe on the floor. "Where is that sound coming from?" When I feel him get up from beside me, I try to raise my arm to point at the front door and my purse, but I can't, so I just close my eyes. The sound of my phone stops two seconds later. "It was your alarm," he says.

"I know. I get up to run," I say, my eyes still closed, and I feel a cool breeze on me. He has taken the cover or sheet off me. "Not today."

"Nah," he says, and I feel his fingers move over my legs softly, and I moan or groan. "Today, I have a whole new exercise for you." My legs open like the big fucking hussy I am. I've never been this into sex in my life. The minute he pulls out of me, I want him back inside me again. He was not lying when he said he was going to fuck me all night long. I think we've slept maybe thirty minutes. "I see someone is happy to see me," he says, and he slips two fingers into me. I'm wet already, knowing what's to come. "Did you miss me?"

"Yes," I say, trying to look over my shoulder, but I can't. My eyes close when I feel him lifting my hips and then burying his face between my legs.

"We are going to try something," he says, and I want to laugh.

"We've tried just about fucking everything you've wanted," I say, moaning as he slips a finger into my ass. "Not that." I close my eyes as he works his finger and tongue into me. The man can do some serious shit with that tongue of his. Things that should be illegal. He was fucking me so hard I thought he was going to break me. But instead, he pulled out and ate me until I came on his tongue and then fucked me again. It was the best sex of my life.

"Not that," he says, stopping. "But." He leans over me and grabs another condom, and I feel the tip of his cock slip into me, and I swear I don't think I've had any-one this large before. His hand grabs my hips as he slams into me again. "You are going to fuck me."

"Turn over," I say and look over my shoulder.

"Oh, no." He shakes his head. "You want my cock, you have to fuck it like you are now." He puts his hands up. "Fuck me back," he says as he pushes me forward, and I push back on him. "That's it, Becca." He doesn't move the next time, so I do all the work. I grab the sheets in my hands as I push back on his cock. I rock forward and back as his hand goes to the side of me. "Fuck me, Becca," he says over and over again. My tits rub the sheets and pucker as they drag across the sheets.

"Nico," I say to him, so close to coming I can feel it. I fuck him back, rocking faster and harder. He gets up on his knees, and he slips a finger into my ass, making me feel full.

"That's it, baby. Fuck me back," he says, and I do. I fuck him back with everything that I have, and when I come on his cock, he comes also. I collapse on my stomach with him on top of me.

"I need to sleep," I say, and he laughs, pulling out of me and getting off the bed. "Come back," I say, and he laughs, going to the bathroom. I hear the water turn on and off, and then I hear the curtains shutting. The room is now pitch black, and he slides in beside me. I feel the covers over me, and he takes me into his arms.

He kisses the back of my neck. "Sleep, baby," he says, and I'm about to answer him, but I fall asleep with a smile on my face.

I turn over and feel for him, but the bed is empty. I get up on my elbow and look at the dark room, seeing that I'm alone. I get out of bed and go to the bathroom, turning on the light enough to see the marks all over my body. His teeth marks are on both tits and on my hip. I wash my hands and then look for a robe but find one of his white T-shirts. I put it over me and walk out to see him sitting down in one of the leather chairs. He is wearing one of the robes as he has his phone to his ear.

"That sounds good," he tells them and opens his arms for me to sit on his lap. I look over and see covered plates on the table. I point toward the table, then walk over to it and pour myself a cup of coffee. My whole body aches when I take a sip and then sit down in the same chair he sat in last night. I put the cup to my lips again to hide the smile when I see my ass cheek mark on the table.

"What is that smile about?" Nico asks when he gets off the phone. He walks over to me, and I see his cock at half-mast. I don't think I've ever seen it not hard before. "Morning." He stops in front of me, and I'm ready to put my cup of coffee down and have his cock in my mouth. But he bends and kisses my lips.

"Hi," I whisper back, holding his head in one of my hands and kissing him one more time. "Morning."

"That look means trouble," he says, sitting down in the chair next to me.

"Well, for one, I thought you were going to let me eat your cock for breakfast." I wink at him as I see his cock spring into action. "Then my ass print is on this table." I point at the table, and I see him laughing.

"I didn't even notice," he says. "I ordered everything on the menu," he says, getting up and closing his robe when his cock comes out. He takes the silver domes off the food. "This we can have later." He winks at me as he moves the bowl of strawberries over to the couch. He then picks up the phone. "Hi, can I get some whipped cream and some chocolate?"

"Two!" I shout at him as he hangs up the phone. "You're not going to have all the fun," I say, and he shakes his head.

We eat breakfast sitting next to each other when there is a knock on the door. He walks over to the door, and I hear voices. "Thank you," he says, closing the door and coming back in carrying the big silver tray.

"They didn't walk it in?" I ask, and he looks at me, walking to the living room area and sets down the tray.

"You're naked," he says, and I look down and see that the T-shirt is semi see-through, but my nipples are pebbled, making it a little bit more see-through than it should be.

I stand. "I'm not naked," I say, putting my hands on my hips. He walks over to me and picks me up around my waist. He carries me over to the desk and puts me down on it. His hand goes into his pocket to grab a condom. My hands stroke his cock, working it with my hand. I'm about to take off the T-shirt when he rips the collar down under one of my tits.

My mouth opens in shock. His arm goes around my waist again, picking me up and slamming me down on his cock. My hands wrap around his neck as he carries us to the couch. He sits down as I straddle him. "Mine," he says, leaning down and taking the nipple into his mouth as I move up and down. His hand goes to my hip as he guides me, and I watch him.

My head falls forward, and I grab his bottom lip between my teeth. His hand squeezes my nipple, sending a shiver down my whole body. "Fuck," he hisses when I squeeze him with my pussy. "How does it get fucking better?"

I laugh, kissing him, and then place my hands on his knees behind me. I fuck him faster. He moves the shirt up and licks his thumb. He plays with my clit, his eyes never coming up again as he watches his cock disappear into me. "Faster," I say, moving my hips, and he flicks it, and I come with his name on my lips. He lets me come down from it. His hands go to my hips, and just like that, I'm picked up and bent over the couch where he fucks me so hard we move the couch. He comes five minutes later, burying himself in me. He slaps my ass when he slips out of me, and I literally walk to the bathroom with my legs spread.

I start the shower and look back at him. "Don't you fucking dare join me," I say, and he laughs.

"I want to wash your back," he says, leaning against the counter, his cock soft again.

"You washed my back last night, and I felt like I was drowning," I say, getting into the shower and looking at him.

"You are the one who bent over," he says while I close my eyes and let the water cascade around my face.

"You were the one who grabbed my hips and pounded into me over and over again. I couldn't even yell for help." He laughs, and so do I.

"Did you have any plans today?" he asks, and I shake my head.

"Honestly, I was staying in New York so I could think about what was happening between us." I can't believe I just laid it out for him. "The whole kiss threw me off, and I thought what better way to clear your head than

New York City."

"You flew to New York City because I kissed you?" he says, shocked. "Where are you going to go now that we had sex?"

"Canada," I say, joking, and he laughs. "How long were you here for?"

"My plane left this morning at eight," he says, and I look at him, shocked. "It's coming back for me on Sunday. I figured I could give you a ride home."

"You stayed here for me?" I ask, not sure I'm ready for the emotion that this declaration brings forth. I'm not sure what the fuck is going on, but what I do know is that I'm not sure I'm ready to give it a name. I don't want to put a label on it. I don't want to put it in any categories as of right now.

"I stayed here because you were here," he admits. "Now, after you finish washing, I'm going to take a shower. Go to your room, pack your stuff, and check out."

"Please," I say, turning off the water and getting out. He hands me a towel, and when I reach for it, he pulls me to him. The towel drops to the floor, and my hands land on his bare chest.

"Get your things, Becca," he says softly and bends his head to kiss me softly. "Please," he whispers before letting me go and stepping into the shower.

"Fine," I say, "but only because you said please." I bring the towel to my mouth to hide my smile, knowing full well I would have done it anyway.

SIXTEEN

Nico

"THERE YOU ARE," I say to Becca when I find her in the little kitchen that the suite has. She is grabbing a bottle of water out of the fridge, opening it, and downing half of it in one gulp.

"Someone is dehydrated." I wink at her, and she rolls her eyes. "The car is here."

"Oh, good," she says, and I take her in. I haven't seen her since she left me in the shower. Her long hair is pinned up in a ponytail, leaving her neck bare for me to kiss it. She's wearing white jeans that look painted on and a thick knitted brown sweater that fits her perfectly.

"That look is going to make the car wait at least thirty minutes." She walks over to me, kissing my lips, and I know if I don't walk away from her, it will be more than thirty minutes. I thought having her right before the car got here would lessen the pull that I have to her. To being with her.

"I've never seen you dressed casual," I say. "I like it." I put my hands around her waist. "A lot."

"I always dress casual when I fly." Her hands go to my waist. "And you are one to talk. Are those sneakers on your feet?" She looks down at my black Nikes, and she laughs. "I don't think I've ever seen you so dressed down."

"You've seen me naked," I point out. "That is the most dressed down I'm going to be."

She throws her head back and laughs, and my cock starts to stir. This weekend with her has been more than I could have ever thought it would be. It was light and easy with no fuss. There was no running out to make sure we were at the best restaurant and to be seen. We walked around the city, holding hands and making out. We spent the nights in bed or around the suite getting lost in each other. I thought after the second day, I would tire of her and want my space, but instead, I craved her touch. I craved to touch her. "Does this plane have a bedroom?"

We walk to the living room, and I pick up my bag as she rolls her suitcase to the door. "I have no idea which one I have today," I say as we make our way down to the car.

When we pull onto the tarmac, I look at the plane. "No bedroom, but there is a living room."

"Oh," she says when I hold out my hand to help her out. "That's too bad."

"Why?" I ask, chuckling.

"The mile-high club is still empty." She winks at me as she walks up the stairs to the plane, leaving me with my own thoughts.

I wait until the bags are loaded before walking up the steps, and I see her sitting on the couch buckled in as she reads something on her phone. "Where did you go?"

"I was trying to get my cock to come down from a salute before getting on the plane." I look over at her, taking a seat next to her. The flight attendant closes the door and tells us we are getting ready for takeoff.

"I could have helped with that," she says, tilting her head, knowing full well if she touches me, the last thing I'm going to be is soft. "You are no fun."

"I'll remember that the next time you beg me to come," I whisper in her ear and bite her earlobe.

"Promises, promises." She baits me just as she always fucking baits me.

For the rest of the flight, we are on our computers working, and for the first time ever, no one gets on my case about working. A lot of times, I'm nagged to take a break but not with Becca. She works just as hard on her computer, and when we land, she puts her computer away. "I have so much work to catch up on."

"Play hard," I say, "work harder."

"I don't think that's the way the saying goes." She laughs, and when we get off the plane, a car is waiting for us. "I can get a ride home if you are too busy."

"You mean that, don't you?" I ask, and she just looks at me confused.

"If it was anyone else …" I say. She walks closer to me, and I love that she doesn't back down. "You mean, if it was another woman, she would be pissed that you fucked her all weekend long and are expecting her to get her own ride home." I laugh. "But I'm not one of those women. For one, I think I fucked you just as much as you fucked me."

"Get in the SUV, Becca," I say, and her eyes twinkle. If I had the time, I'd bring her back to my house and fuck her a couple more times.

"What do we say?" She folds her arms over her chest. "You can do it."

"Please," I say between clenched teeth, and she claps her hands together, walking toward the SUV.

I give the driver her address, and my heart beats a bit erratically when we pull up to her building. "Well, Nico," she says, turning and looking at me, and she is beautiful. Every single day, she gets more beautiful. "Thank you for a wonderful weekend."

"Why the fuck do I feel like I'm being dismissed?" I grab her and bring her to me. "I'll call you later." Her eyes change from the light to a dark, and I kiss her. Her mouth opens for me as our tongues meet again. We kiss until the door opens, and she slips out of my arms.

The doorman welcomes her home, and she smiles at him. She walks into the building with the man beside her as she rolls her luggage. She never once looks back, making me miss her even more.

I walk into my own house twenty minutes later, dumping my bag on the table in the middle of the room. "Welcome home." I look up to see Lizzie standing on the second floor, leaning against the railing.

"Hey," I say to her, picking up the paper she left for

me there.

The door opens to the left as she gets out of the elevator. "How lazy did that make me look?"

"You would have been here faster if you took the stairs." I laugh and look up at her. She just watches me as I walk toward the kitchen. "Did you leave me any food?" I look over my shoulder, knowing she always raids my fridge when I'm gone.

"If you are asking me if I touched your disgusting healthy meals," she says, sitting on one of the stools at the counter. "That would be a no."

I laugh, pulling open the fridge and grabbing a black plastic bowl to pop into the microwave. Lizzie has gotten up and is making herself a coffee. She looks over at me. "How was New York?"

"Good," I say, not giving her any details.

"Did you end up meeting Laurene while you were there?" I shake my head as I eat. "Are you telling me that you stayed in New York all weekend long with Becca?"

"I'm not telling you anything." I don't look over at her. I'm not ready for this conversation with her. I'm not ready to share whatever I had with Becca with anyone.

"Oh my God," she says, slapping the counter. "You have lost your mind."

"Why do you say that?" I ask, confused.

"You had sex with Becca," she says, and I don't confirm it. "Do you really think that was the best decision?"

"I don't know what it has to do with anything," I say, ignoring the burning in my stomach.

"It has to do with the fact you guys work together,"

she says. "How is that going to work?"

"Number one, we don't work together." Lizzie's face says it all. "Okay, we work together sometimes."

"Seven," Lizzie says to me. "She is the agent to seven players on your team."

"And?" I say, shocked that I didn't know that.

"I just think that there is a line in the sand, and you crossed it," she says, and I shrug my shoulders. "So what happens now?"

"Nothing," I say. "I'm here. She's there." I ignore the pang of missing her.

"So you guys are going to what, pretend you haven't done the nasty with each other every single time?" She takes a sip of her coffee. "It's going to be awkward."

"It's only awkward if you make it that way. We are two consenting adults who spent the weekend together. No one needs to know anything more than that."

"It's going to get messy," she says. "Then what?"

I shrug, not ready to face all those questions, because I'm scared of what the answers are going to be. "How is Laurene?"

"She's good," she says. "She really needs to speak to you."

I look over at her with the way her tone was. "Is she okay?" I ask, and she gets off the stool.

"That is for me to know and you to find out," she says to me. "Off the record."

I look at her now. "You look happy."

"What does that mean?" I ask. "I'm always happy."

"No." She shakes her head. "You always pretend to

be happy. Smile when you need to. Say what needs to be said." I just look at her. "Maybe it won't be so bad."

"What does that mean?" I ask.

"It means that if she makes you happy, go for it." I don't say anything to her, not sure what to say. "Just be wary."

"I've never not been wary," I say, getting up and tossing out the rest of the meal. Suddenly, I'm not hungry anymore. "You know me," I say, turning and leaning against the counter to look at her.

"I do know you," she says. "I just don't want you to get hurt in all of this."

"Look, I don't know what to say right now," I say. "Becca came out of the blue. You know this. She was never on my radar."

"And now she is." She points at me.

"And now she is," I admit. "It was one weekend," I finally say out loud, not adding in that it was one fucking amazing weekend. The best that I've ever had. I don't add any of that because I'm not ready. And when I am ready, I think that I should talk to Becca about it and not Lizzie. "When it becomes more than that."

She smirks at me. "It'll be fun to watch." She turns, walking away. "Call Laurene!" she shouts.

SEVENTEEN

BECCA

"ERIKA," I SAY when I walk out of my office, "can you make sure that all of these are mailed out?" I hand her the box of holiday cards that I just finished signing. "Also," I start to tell her, but I hear his voice, and my head turns to see Nico walking in with Francis. They are joking about something, and he looks up, seeing me. His smile turns into a smirk. "Well, well, well," I say, walking to them, "what do we have here?" I look at him, seeing him in a charcoal suit. The black button-down shirt hides the six-pack I know is under there. His belt locking up his best feature. His hair is pushed back, and I try not to think about how I held on to his hair or the way it felt between my legs.

"Hello," Nico says. I don't know why, but something gets me not to kiss his lips and wish him hello the way I want to. "Just the woman I wanted to see." It's been four days since I've seen him or spoken to him. I am not going to lie. I have been checking my phone more often than I should lately.

"Here I am?" I say to him, putting my hands in front of me instead of slipping my finger into his.

"Excuse me, you two," Francis says. "I have a meeting in five minutes."

I wait for Francis to step away before I look back at Nico. "Please come this way," I say, leading him back to my office, smiling at Erika, who looks up at us. "So," I say, walking to my desk, turning in time to see him close the door behind him.

He walks to me, his eyes going dark as he gets close to me. "Hi," he says, putting his arm around my waist. "You look good."

"Had I known you were coming, I would have dre—" I'm stopped when his lips land on mine. My mouth opens for his, and for the first time in four days, I feel okay. Instead of that feeling I was missing something or forgetting something, everything I need is right here. My hands go into the hair I was just thinking about. He kisses me until I'm breathless, and when he lets me go, it takes a minute for me to open my eyes.

"You look good enough to eat," he says, and I tilt my head to the side.

"Must be the shoes," I say about my shiny black Louboutin shoes.

"It's the whole fucking package," he says, grabbing my ass with one hand and pushing me into him to show me how hard he is.

"We can't do this here," I say, taking all my courage

and stepping away from him. "This is my workplace." I shake my head, and he just smiles. "Which means it's off-limits for anything until after five."

"Good to know," he says. "But I didn't come here for that."

"Oh?" I ask, surprised.

"I just got back. We were on the West Coast for three days," he says, and I want to ask if his phone works on the West Coast. I want to ask him why he didn't call, but then again, why didn't I call him?

"And I was your first stop," I tease him, walking back to him. "Isn't that sweet?"

"Yes," he says, putting his hands in his pockets. "Actually, I came to personally invite you to the team Christmas party."

I laugh. "The one that is tomorrow?" I ask. "In less than twenty-four hours."

"That would be the one," he says, and I shake my head.

"What's the matter? Did your date cancel on you at the last minute?" I try to joke about it, but it bothers me more than I thought it would.

"I missed you," he says softly. "And I wanted to see you."

"I have to check my phone," I say, walking over to my desk. And I pick it up and call him. He looks at his phone and then up at me. "Oh, so my phone works, and so does yours."

He laughs, getting what I'm getting at. I'm expecting him to hang up, but instead, he answers it. "Hey, beautiful."

"Smooth," I say, my eyes never leaving his. "Very, very smooth."

"Sorry I haven't called you," he says, "but I've been in LA for three days, and it's been crazy." His voice goes lower.

"I'm glad you're back," I say to him both on the phone and in person.

"Are you busy tomorrow?" he asks, and I shake my head. "Good. Party is at seven. I'll send you all the details."

"Okay," I say.

"I have a dinner tonight, or I'd ask you to come with me."

"I'm busy tonight," I lie, and I can see his eyes asking me with who.

"Tomorrow it is," he says softly. "Can I kiss you before I leave?"

"Would it matter if I said no?" I ask, laughing when he shakes his head. He walks to me, and I set my phone down.

"I'll see you tomorrow," he says, moving my hair over my shoulder. "I really wish I got here after five."

"Is that so?" I ask him. "And what would you do if you got here after five?"

"I'd fuck you right on your desk," he says without thinking twice. "The only thing is you'd have to keep quiet."

I laugh. "I believe I heard you roar my name a couple of times."

"I have to go," he says, and I meet his lips for a kiss. I watch him leave, sitting down in my chair and letting out a breath I didn't know I was holding.

"Did you need me for anything?" Erika says to me five minutes later. "I was going to head out to the post office."

I look at my watch, seeing it's just after three thirty. "Why don't you go ahead and call it a day? Early weekend."

"Thank you," she says. "I also have all the travel information for you for next month."

"God, I hate January and February," I say.

"You say that every single year," she says, "as soon as December starts."

"Well then, consider me a creature of habit," I say, and she laughs. I stay at my desk until eight, going over the travel schedule.

My phone beeps with a message.

Nico: I'm looking forward to seeing you tomorrow.

I don't answer him that night or the next day either. I slip on my red heels when I get a call that my car is waiting. Taking one more look at my outfit, I ignore the flutters in my stomach.

The red skirt is tight around my waist and flares out. It looks like a bell shirt going to my knees. The top is what makes it sexy, a lace spaghetti strap tight top. The red heels make the whole outfit. My hair is loose and in long waves, tied to one side with a diamond pin. I grab the black shawl, walking to the car. The driver opens the door for me as soon as he sees me.

I make sure my red lipstick is on when we arrive at the address that I was given. The sound of music floats through the air from the restaurant. My door is opened by one of the valets. "Thank you," I say to him and walk into the restaurant.

"Can I take your jacket?" A woman comes to me, and I hand her my shawl. "I'll be back with your ticket," she says, and I wait here until she gets back. The whole place is shut down for this event. Christmas trees are in every corner. The logo of the team is in every single place that there isn't a Christmas decoration. Christmas carols are playing as I look around the room to see if I spot anyone that I know.

"Becca." I hear my name and look over to see Ryder, one of the assistant coaches, coming over to me. He's wearing a gray suit, and he kisses me on the cheek. "So nice of you to come."

"Thank you," I say, and then another waitress comes over with a tray full of eggnog and champagne. I grab a glass of champagne. "This is a nice spot." I make conversation, and he smiles and looks down. I think he's nervous, but I'm not sure.

"Hey." I hear from beside me and turn to see Manning walking in. "You're here," he says, and I smile at him.

"I'm here." I take a sip of my drink while he looks over at Ryder and nods. I look around the room to see if Nico is here. I see a couple of players that I represent. "I'm going to go say hi to Jake and Patrick," I tell Manning. "Save me a seat beside you."

I walk around people, smiling and then stop by Jake

and kiss his cheek, and I do the same to Patrick. "Becca," Patrick says, "you are looking beautiful as always."

"Well, thank you," I say. We talk about the holidays and how happy he is that his family is coming in from Canada. I'm in the middle of talking to him when I feel a hand on my back, and I turn to see Miller standing there. "Hello, you," I say, and I turn to hug him. "You look nice."

"Thank you," he says, and I look over his shoulder for Layla. "Where is your better half?"

"I'm right here," she says from beside him. "You look fabulous," she says, looking at my outfit. "I love this skirt." She then looks at Miller. "Where is my phone?"

"In my pocket," he says, looking at her, "and you aren't getting it until Monday."

"Miller Adams, I will," she says, and I laugh.

"I'm going to go get a fresh drink," I say. "Do you want one?" I ask Layla, and she smiles and nods her head. I walk to the bar and place my empty glass down on the wooden bar.

"What can I get you?" the bartender asks.

"Whatever she has is on me," Ryder says from beside me, and I laugh, and so does he. "It's actually all on Nico."

"Well, in that case," I say, "I'll have two glasses of wine." Ryder just looks at me. "One is for Layla."

He leans one hand on the bar. "Tell me, Becca, why haven't we spent more time together?" I look at him and throw my head back and laugh.

"I'm going to go out on a limb and say because I don't

mix business with pleasure," I say, trying not to tell him that the other reason that I won't go out with him is because I have never thought of him in that way.

"How about we bend the rules for once?" he says, and then he leans in closer. "Take a chance, Becca," he says.

"What's going on over here?" I feel a hand on my back. This time my whole body lights up from his touch.

"I'm trying to convince Becca to bend the rules and let me take her out," Ryder says, and I look over at Nico.

"Is that so?" he says.

"It is so," I say as the bartender sets the two glasses of wine on the bar for me. "Thank you so much." I step forward to grab the two glasses, and my back still feels the heat from where his hand was. "If you gentlemen will excuse me, Layla looks like she needs a drink."

"Let me help you," Nico says, grabbing a glass from me. "Lead the way."

EIGHTEEN

Nico

WALKING INTO THE holiday party, I shake Manning's hand and then Miller's, who's standing next to him. I do a sweep of the room and see her right away.

She's standing at the bar with Ryder, who is leaning into her. I don't even bother with the conversation going on in front of me. I walk over to her. I texted her last night, and she never got back to me. I don't know why the fuck it bothered me, but it did. I checked my phone a ridiculous amount of times while I was at dinner, and to be honest, I have no idea what was even going on.

I was gone for four days without talking to her or seeing her, and the minute that I saw her, I missed her more than I cared to admit.

"What's going on over here?" I put my hand on the base of her back. Her body has a slight shiver.

I look at Becca and then Ryder. "I'm trying to convince Becca to bend the rules and let me take her out."

Ryder smirks and then looks over at me. The only thing I can see in my head is me throat punching him.

"Is that so?" It is the only thing I can muster up to say, putting my hands in my pockets before I throat punch him accidentally.

"It is so," Becca says right before the bartender sets two glasses of wine on the bar. "Thank you so much. If you gentlemen will excuse me, Layla looks like she needs a drink."

"Let me help you." I grab a glass from her, and she just looks at me. "Lead the way."

She walks past me, and I smell her soft citrus smell, and my cock stirs for her. "Here you are," Becca says, handing the glass to Layla.

"Thank you," she says, and they click glasses. I put my hands in my pockets before I reach out for her. It's not the time for me to do anything rash.

"There you are," Lizzie says, coming to me. She looks at everyone and says hello. "Hello, everyone. It's time for pictures."

"It's my favorite time of the night," Manning says, and I laugh at him as he follows Lizzie. I look over at Becca, who just looks at me as I follow Lizzie.

I walk over to where Lizzie is, and my eyes fly back to see Becca chatting with the girls. Her head goes back as she laughs. I look forward again, but I'm aware of where she is every single minute that we are doing pictures.

There are waiters that go up to her, and she smiles at them, and they are all under her spell, and she has no idea. Her hair is to one side, leaving her neck out and open for me to bite it. I pose for a picture, my eyes always roaming the room to see her walking around.

When the photographer says he has everything he needs, I look around the room again. This time I see her asking the waitress something, and I see her pointing at the darkened hall. I walk behind her without her knowing, and I grab her by the hips right before she is about to go into the bathroom. She shrieks out. "You are driving me crazy," I bend and whisper in her ear, and she turns around.

"I haven't even done anything." She looks up at me. I look from right to left, seeing a brown door. I grab her hand, opening the door and seeing it's a maintenance closet. Pulling her in behind me and turning so I can close the door behind her, I push her against the door.

"Do you know that red is a color for sex?" My hands go to her face. "I missed you," I admit.

"Is that so?" She smirks, my mouth coming closer to hers. "I missed you, too," she admits to me right before our mouths meet. She arches her back into me, and my cock stirs to life. She moves her hands from her sides to my hips, then down to cup my cock. We swallow each other's moans.

"Fuck," I say, leaving her lips and sucking on her neck. She raises her leg over my hip, pressing her pussy to my cock. "We can't do this here." I move from one side of her neck to the other. My hands go up to her ass and bunch the skirt into my fists.

"You're right." Her voice comes out in almost a pant. "We can't do this." She moves her hand up and down on my cock. I feel her hands on the zipper. "We should get out there," she says, moving her hand into my pants. Her hand creeps to the elastic of my boxers, and just like that, her soft smooth hand is holding my cock.

"I have to get inside you." My hands move to her skirt and pull it up until it's around her waist. Her hands go to my belt as she unclips it at the same time I push her thong to the side and slide two fingers into her. "Too long." I say the only thing that comes to my head.

She pushes the pants over my hips as my cock springs free. "This isn't how I wanted to do this," I say, reaching into my back pocket and pulling out a condom. I look at her through the dark, her eyes closed as she moves her hips with my fingers.

"More." Her hand moves in sync with my fingers.

"I wanted you spread out for me." I push her hands away from my cock as I roll the condom down over my cock. I have a moment of what the fuck am I doing going through my head. But it's only for a split second because the need to have her is bigger than any doubt that I have right now. I pick her leg up over my arm, opening her as wide as she can go, replacing my fingers with my cock. Both of us moaning when I slide all the way in. "We don't have time." I thrust into her as hard as I can, and she moans out louder. "Shhh," I say, my thrusts coming harder and shorter.

We both hear voices coming closer to the door as my thrusts go slower. Inch by fucking inch coming out of her and then slamming back into her. I feel her fingers moving over her clit. "Nico," she says my name, and I know she's about to come because my cock is being strangled by her. "So close."

"Let go," I say, putting my mouth on hers as she comes. I swallow down her silent moan right before I push myself balls deep in her, and I close my eyes. I come for what seems like hours. I haven't had her in four days, and I've been dying. I've woken up every single morning with the biggest hard-on, and nothing, I mean nothing could cure it. I had to take care of myself every single day, but it wasn't the same.

Her tongue slowly lets go of mine, our chests heaving. "That was so needed," she says, kissing under my jaw. "Thank you for that."

I slip out of her, and my arm drops her leg. "Come home with me." I say the words before my mind can catch up to what is happening. My house is always off-limits. It's the only place that is truly only mine. I've never brought a woman home, and not only was I asking her to come over but I was also planning on not letting her leave until she had to.

"What?" she asks, almost as shocked as I am. I tuck myself back into my pants.

"Come home with me," I say again, this time I'm not sure I'm asking her. "I'll see you out there." Kissing her and walking out to go to the bathroom, I'm thankful that no one is there so I slip into the men's bathroom and take care of the condom. I wash my hands before pulling the door open and seeing Ryder joking with Becca.

"Totally wrong door," she says and looks at me. "They need a brighter light in the hallway."

"Is everything okay?" I ask, and Ryder laughs.

"Becca walked into the wrong door," he says as Becca's smile never leaves her face.

"Well, excuse me while I visit the actual ladies' room," she says to both of us as she walks away and goes to the bathroom.

"That woman," Ryder says once Becca is out of earshot. "I've been trying to get her to notice me for a year now."

"I had no idea," I say, putting my hands in my pockets and not making any attempt to leave the hallway. "I think she's with someone."

He looks at me in surprise. "Really?" he says and I have no other words to say right now. "She is always alone."

"I think she mentioned it to me the other day." I am lying out of my ass right now.

Becca comes out and stops when she sees us both here. "Are you guys waiting for me?" she asks, and I swear she glows.

"I was just chatting with Ryder here." I look at him. "I bet him fifty bucks you had a boyfriend."

Her eyes go wide. "Is that so?" She folds her arms over her chest. "I don't know if you would call him my boyfriend," she says. "More like a friend with a certain benefit. We haven't really put a name on it."

"Well then, it's his loss," Ryder says. "Shall we?" He motions with his hand. Becca walks out into the party with both of us following her.

"I think it's time to sit," Ryder says.

"I have to find Manning." Becca looks over at him. "We are sitting together."

"Well then, I will see you later," he tells her as we both look around for Manning, and I see him sitting at a table with Ralph and Miller.

"It's time." I look up to see Lizzie there, and my eyebrows pinch together. "The speech. You know welcome, have fun, Merry Christmas, all that jazz."

"Right," I say, taking a huge breath of air, looking to see her sitting as she takes a sip of wine. "Where am I sitting?" I ask Lizzie, who looks around the room and then looks back at me.

"Where would your highness like to sit?" she asks sarcastically. "I think I see two chairs empty at Manning's table. Would you like me to reserve them for us?"

I glare at her. "That would be good." She shakes her head, laughing. "Go say your speech. I hope you aren't this grumpy during dinner." She looks over her shoulder, walking away. "Something tells me you are going to be super chipper."

"You're fired," I say between clenched teeth.

"Good." She smiles back at me. "If you want to rehire me, I need a new contract." She turns. "I'll ask Becca if she'll take me on as a client."

I'm about to tell her to fuck off when Martin approaches. "I'm ready when you are." He looks at me.

"I'll start." Turning to walk to the DJ booth. "Let's get this over with so we can eat," I say, but in reality, I just want to get to my seat.

NINETEEN

BECCA

"How are you enjoying Dallas?" I ask Graham when I finally catch him.

"I'm loving it, actually," he says, smiling. "The team was amazing in welcoming me. From Nico to the coach and even the players. Every person has been helpful."

"I'm so, so glad," I say. "Now, it's time to put your money where your mouth is and show them what you can really do."

"That's my goal," he says, and I have no doubt he'll make sure he kills it. He is looking to score big with his next contract, and I'm going to do what I need to do on my end to do just that.

"If I can have everyone's attention." I hear Nico's voice boom over the system. The chatter of everyone comes to a stop. The sounds of plates fill the room as they start to serve the first course. "If everyone can get to their seats. Dinner will be starting," he says as people move to their respective seats. I tap Graham's arm, walking over to the table and sitting next to Manning. The two chairs beside me are empty.

"I wanted to take a minute to thank you guys for all of the hard work that everyone is doing this year. It hasn't been an easy year so far." He points at a guy sitting in a wheelchair. "But I have no doubt with our newest member"—he points at Graham, who just nods at him—"we are going to be kicking ass. Your coach wants to say a little something." He hands the mic to the coach, and I zone out, mostly because all I can do is look at Nico. His black suit molds to him, and I can see his smooth chest where his white button-down shirt is open at the neck. A chest I licked to my heart's content last weekend. Whether he was on top of me or I was riding him, I made sure I left my mark on him.

"Is anyone sitting here?" Lizzie asks Miller of the empty seat beside him, and she sits down and smiles at me.

"Okay, folks, drink and be merry," Nico says. I look over at Lizzie, and we share a confused look.

I know the minute the empty seat beside me is being pulled out that he is sitting right next to me. I knew the minute Lizzie came to sit at the table that he would follow.

I side-eye him as he takes a drink from a glass of water. He moves to the side, closer to me when the man places a plate in front of him.

"That was a fine speech," Lizzie says to him. "I like how you said drink and get merry. That was an interesting choice of words." Nico looks at her, and I can feel his leg beside mine.

I roll my lips together, trying not to laugh at her. "That is how the saying goes. Drink and be merry." He starts to argue with her and looks around the table. Layla is the only one willing to tell him the truth.

"I don't think so," Layla says while I lean back in my chair.

"I'm going to check Google," Miller says, and we all groan.

"Is there anything that you don't check on Google?" I ask, and Layla answers for him, rolling her eyes.

"Nope." She looks over at him. "He googles just about everything. Last week, he had to google what was an appropriate Christmas gift for a girlfriend of one year."

"You did not," I say, slapping the table while Ralph and Manning just shake their heads and laugh at him.

"I did, and I'll have you know I didn't take any of their suggestions." He looks back at Layla. "I went out of my bubble. It is a saying, 'Eat, drink, and be merry.'"

Nico looks over at Lizzie. "Told you so," he says to her.

"Let me finish," Miller says, and we all look over at him. "For tomorrow we die."

"What?" Ralph says out loud, gasping. "Shut up. That isn't true."

"It is," he says, handing him the phone, and he passes it around the table. Nico is the only one to pass on looking at it. I lean over him to hand Lizzie the phone.

"This is a classic, and I'm never going to let you live

it down." She looks at Nico. "Miller, while you are on Google," Lizzie says, grabbing her glass of wine and finishing it off, "can you check and see if red is the color for sex?"

"It is," Manning says. "It has to be." I look over at him.

"Told you," Lizzie says, clapping her hands together and pointing at Nico.

"It is not," I say, shaking my head. "It's actually a mating tactic for other species." I take a sip of wine.

"So it's a yes," Miller says. "It says a female wears red as a sexual signal."

"Are we having a debate?" I ask, looking at the women. "I'm wearing red tonight. I'm not on the hunt to attract a male."

"That's not what I heard," Candace says teasingly, pointing at me. "I heard Ryder was asking about you."

I look over at her, shocked, avoiding Nico's stare. "He asked me about you." Ralph puts up his hand.

"Me, too," Manning says, looking over at me.

"Me, too," Nico says from beside me, and I look over at him.

"Well, I'm very much not available," I tell the table, side-eyeing Nico. "Besides, what's the saying." I look at Miller. "Don't shit where you eat."

"Yes." Miller points at me, cutting his steak. "Obviously, I didn't listen to that." He looks over at Layla and winks.

"I didn't either," Ralph says, pulling Candace to him and kissing her lips.

"Well, unlike you two," I say, "I know how to follow the rules."

"I need another drink," Lizzie says, getting up. "Anyone want anything?"

"Shots," Layla says, "for the girls."

Miller pushes away from the table and holds out his hand to Layla. "Come dance with me." She smiles at him shyly and grabs his hand, going to the dance floor. Ralph and Candace follow, and I feel Manning push away from the table.

"If you ask me to dance, I'm going to kick you in the balls," I tell Manning, side-eyeing him while I cut a piece of my food and chew it.

"I'm not going to ask you to dance," he says, laughing. "I'm actually ducking out."

"Ohhh, does this have to do with …?" I ask, not sure what Nico knows.

"It totally does. I wanted to bring her today, but she was against it," Manning says. "So if it's okay with you," he tells Nico.

"I'll tell them the sitter called," Nico says, covering for him. "Go have fun."

I watch him walk out of the restaurant and then look over at Nico, who sits in the chair and puts his arm over my chair. His thumb rubs up and down my shoulder. "Is that what you and Ryder were talking about?" I ask Nico. "He asked you about me."

"More or less," he says, picking up his glass of water, his hand never leaving my arm.

"What did you tell him?" I ask, looking at him. When

he took me in the closet before, I was shocked that I let it happen. Shocked that I would be that crazy to getting caught with my pants down or my skirt up. But with one touch, I melted in his arms.

"I told him you were taken," he says, drinking and avoiding my eyes.

"Did you?" I look at him and wait for his gaze to meet mine.

"I might have mentioned you were seeing someone on the down low," he says and looks at me. "When do you want to leave?"

"We haven't even eaten," I point out.

"I have food at home," he says, leaning in. "Besides, I had a different meal in mind anyway."

"Did you?" I'm about to ask what exactly that means when everyone comes back.

"I have shots." Lizzie sets down a tray and hands it to the women. "Bottoms up, ladies." She hands me a shot, and I put my hand up and down the tequila shot.

It burns all the way down. I cough a little, setting the glass down. "Well, everyone, that is my cue to leave before I make a really bad decision," I say, getting up. "Thank you for the invite, Nico," I say. "Everyone, I'll see you soon." I turn, walking to the door, getting my ticket out for my shawl.

The woman takes off to get me my shawl, and she's back within minutes. "Ready?" I hear Nico beside me, and my eyes go wide. "I told them I had a business meeting I had to attend."

"They believed you?" I ask, shocked as he puts his

hand on the base of my back.

"Lizzie knew exactly why I was leaving," he says, and I don't know why I'm shocked by this. I saw her in New York, and then he stayed with me.

"My driver," I say, and he looks at me.

"I should go and get my car and maybe change clothes," I say, and he smirks at me.

"The plans I have for you." He gets even closer to me. "Involves you with no clothes on." My car comes around, and the driver gets out. "She's taken care of," Nico says, grabbing my hand and pulling me toward his SUV.

He puts me in the passenger seat before going to his side of the SUV. He gets in, and just the way he handled that makes me so hot for him. I've never had someone take charge like that. They usually let me do my own thing. It's what I've always wanted, what I've always thought I wanted. I was wrong. "I don't like being told what to do," I say, and he looks over at me, smirking.

"You're lying," he says, pulling out of the parking lot. One hand is on the steering wheel, and one is on the door. The black suit fits his arm so perfectly. The cuffs stick out perfectly, the monogram engraved on his cuff links. "If I wasn't driving right now." He looks at me. "I'd show you just how much you love me telling you what to do."

"Don't flatter yourself," I say, looking out the window, afraid that if he sees my eyes, he will know I'm lying.

I can't even focus on the ride there, my mind is playing everything that I want him to do to me. I cross my legs when I think of how he took me in a fucking closet. "What's the matter?" I look over at him.

"Why do you think something is the matter?" I ask, pretending my body isn't affected by him.

"You love when I'm the boss," he says, and I roll my eyes. He pushes a button, and the gate opens. I look at his monster of a house and any other time I would be more interested in it. But right now my body has a really big itch and he's the only one that can scratch it. "How much do you want to bet if I slide my fingers inside you," he says, unbuckling his seat belt and then leaning over, "you'll be soaking?"

I look at him, turning in my seat and I'm thankful this SUV is spacious. My back against the door, I put one leg on the dashboard and cock the other one up. I pull my dress up showing him that nothing will stop him from entering me. "Only one way to find out," I bait him.

TWENTY

NICO

"WHERE ARE YOU going?" I lift my head off the pillow and see Becca getting out of bed. I turn my head to see that it is just after five in the morning. "The sun isn't even up yet." I turn over on my back to watch and see where she is going. She walks over to the chair in the corner and grabs her clothes.

"I know." She laughs over her shoulder as she puts on the black lace top that she wore two days ago. "But it's Monday morning, and I have work." She grabs the red dress and slips into it. "Go back to sleep," she whispers.

"I can drive you." I had the weekend off, which never really happens. After we got home from the party on Friday, we stayed in my bedroom for a good twenty-four hours without coming out. The both of us frantic to one-up the other person. I've never had this need before. I've never had this want before. "At seven."

"I really need to get a run in." She walks back over to

the corner picking up her shoes. "I haven't worked out all weekend."

"I beg to differ." Tossing the sheets off me and getting up. As naked as the day I was born.

"Naked Twister is not exercise." She laughs, grabbing her bag. "What are you doing getting up? I can get an Uber."

"And I can drive you," I say, walking to her and grabbing her face, giving her a kiss. Her hands land on my hips. "You are wearing too much clothes," I say when I pull her to me.

"God." Her breath comes out in a whisper when I start to kiss her neck. "I was hoping to avoid this." Her hands go from my hips to my cock. "I guess I could spare a couple of minutes." I try not to laugh, with her there is nothing that lasts a couple of minutes. Nothing. It's always one trying to outlast the other. "But I really have to leave by seven." I don't answer her because she drops to her knees and takes my cock into her mouth. I watch her take me into her mouth, her hand going under her skirt.

The same skirt that she pulled up in the car and baited me. The minute I saw her bare without panties, my face planted into her and I ate her like someone who hadn't eaten in a week. If the SUV had enough room, I would have fucked her right then and there. I thought about going into the back, but after having her in a closet I wanted her spread eagle for me. My hips move as she slowly rolls her tongue over the tip. "Becca," I whisper. She closes her eyes, her mouth moving faster and faster, and I know that she's close herself. I pull my cock out of her mouth, and she groans.

"Get naked," I say, stroking my cock that is still wet from her mouth. She pulls the skirt over her head, and when the skirt is in a puddle around her feet, she steps toward the bed.

She looks over her shoulder. "Think you can give it to me so hard I feel you all day." She baits me again as she bends over, spreading her legs for me. She's already dripping wet, so I grab another condom. When I walk back to her, she has two fingers inside her while her thumb plays with her clit. I place my cock at her entrance, her fingers coming out as I slam into her so hard my balls slap her clit. I hold her hips into my hand so tight I know I'm going to leave a mark as I fuck her with everything that I have.

She puts her knees on the bed and arches her back. I grab her hair, pulling her back to me, and suck her neck. Her nipples are asking for me to hold onto them. I move my hips, fucking her softly, her pussy squeezing me tighter and tighter. I roll both her nipples in my hands and then pitch them. She moans out as she fucks me back, pushing against me. "Hold on," I say and she places her hand onto the bed as I slam into her over and over again. The both of us panting and moaning. A thin sheen of sweat fills my chest and her back. "How is it." I slam into her once and slowly pull out . "That I'm still in you." I repeat the same time again. "Yet I can't wait to have you again."

"Fuck," she says one word and I slam into her. "If I know," she says while I pull out slowly. Every single time she gets close, I change the speed. "Nico."

"I don't only want you to feel me." I slide into her so slow I feel every single inch of her hot pussy. "I want you to crave me."

"Make me come," she begs. I grab her ass cheeks, pulling her to me. "Please." The last word comes out in a gasp as I slam back into her. Her eyes close, and this time, I let her come. One after another, she comes on my cock. When she goes over the third time, so do I.

"What are you still doing here?" Becca asks when she steps out of her walk-in closet. After I had her on the bed, I also had her in the shower. I got dressed and drove her home and instead of just going to the office, I went to get her coffee and breakfast. She was shocked when I rang the door fifteen minutes later, and I'm going to honest, she wasn't the only one.

"I'm going to wait until you are ready to leave," I say as she puts on one of her shoes. She went with pants today and a white sweater. It drives me crazy or maybe it just makes me want to puff out my chest when I think about all the marks she has on her.

"No skirt today?" I ask, and she side-eyes me. "What?"

"My knees have carpet burn," she says, and I laugh. "You can go now." She gets up, grabbing her purse and the coffee.

"Are you ready?" I ask and the both of us walk out of her place. Grabbing her hand as we walk down the hallway to her car, I kiss her and put her in her car, only walking to mine when I see her take off.

Twenty minutes later, I'm walking into my office.

Lizzie is at her desk and she lookslook up at me. "Well, if it isn't Casanova." I laugh at her, walking into my office. "I came to see you on Sunday but …" I look over at her. "It sounded like a herd of cattle were mating, so I walked right back out."

"You should have called," I say with a smile.

"You should not be having sex in the kitchen. Things can get burned," she says, and I look over at her.

"Are you speaking from experience?" I tease her.

"Unlike you and your girlfriend, I like to keep everything away from flames," she says and I stop in my tracks with the title she just gave Becca. "Laurene wants you to call her back. It's urgent."

"How is it I go two years without talking to her, and all of a sudden, she wants to speak to me daily?" I ask Lizzie.

"Well, there was a development, and she needs your help," Lizzie tells me. "So call her back."

"I will," I say, picking up my phone and calling her.

"Jesus," she says as soon as she picks up the phone, "you would think I was trying to get in touch with the president." She laughs.

"Sorry, I took the weekend off," I say, looking down at the papers in front of me.

"You took the weekend off?" she shrieks. "You never take the weekend off. Last year, we were in Capri, and you worked from the boat."

"Number one," I start. "It was July first, and that is the trade deadline. Second, I haven't had a day off in forever."

"Two weeks ago in New York," she counters, and I get a bit aggravated now.

"Is that what was so urgent that I had to call you?" I ask. "Seventeen missed calls for that?"

"Actually, ass," she says, "I called to go over the pitch I was going to give today, but since you were MIA, I called Lizzie."

"Oh, good, is this for the company we spoke about?" I ignore her last comment.

"It is," she tells me. "I'm super nervous about it."

"You'll do great," I say, and she breathes out a huge breath.

"I hope so. I know they are a family run company," she says.

"You'll kill it," I say. "You always do. Call me and let me know how it goes."

"Will do," she says and hangs up the phone, my mind forgetting about the conversation five seconds after another call comes in.

I'm in and out of meetings all day long, and when I finally look at the clock, I see it's past seven. "I'm headed home," Lizzie says, peeking her head into the office. "Do you want me to get you something to eat on the way home?"

"No." I shake my head. "I'm good." She nods and leaves and I pick up my phone calling Becca.

"Hello," she says, her voice almost breathless.

"What are you doing?" I ask into the phone.

"I'm on the treadmill," she says, and I laugh. "Got home at five and figured why not."

"You didn't call me today." I get up and walk out of my office.

"Was I supposed to?" she asks. "I'm almost done. How about I call you back?"

She hangs up the phone, and twenty-five minutes later, she hasn't called me back. I get out of my SUV, walking into her building, and the doorman asks who I'm here for.

He has me sign in, and when I knock on the door, there is no answer. I knock again and nothing. I take my phone out and call her. "Hey, sorry," she says. "I took a shower."

"I'm outside your door," I say, and I hear her walking, and the door swings open, and there she stands in a robe and her hair tied at the top of her head. "I brought you dinner." She looks at me in shock as she smiles. She moves back to give me a chance to walk into the place. I lean down and kiss her lips.

"Are we talking real food here," she asks, shutting the door, "or are we talking dick?"

I laugh at her, holding up the bag in my hand. "I mean real food," I say, "but I'm okay with the blow job part." She throws her head back and laughs.

"You would be." She comes to me and wraps her arms around my neck. Going on her tippy toes, she says, "By the way, in case I forget to tell you later. I'm really happy you stopped by."

TWENTY-ONE

BECCA

"WELL, IN CASE I don't tell you later," he says softly as I look up at him. "I'm really happy I came here." He kisses me so softly, if my eyes weren't open, I would've thought it didn't happen.

"Let's go eat." I turn and lead him down the hall into the kitchen. "You bought it, so let me plate it," I say. "Take off your jacket." I watch him as he takes off the jacket I observed him putting on this morning.

I tried to sneak out this morning when I got up, but the minute he felt the bed move, he woke up. I didn't want the whole scene of me leaving and having it awkward, so I tried to sneak out. I can't even explain it. I spent the whole weekend with him naked in his apartment. Getting dressed or actually covered for thirty minutes. We were naked and making out every single time. I felt as if we were trying to get our fill before talking about what this thing really was. Or asking if we are going to actually put a label on it.

"How was your day, dear?" I grab two plates, bringing them back to the brown bag that he brought in.

"Uneventful," he says, taking off his cuff links and rolling up his sleeves. "What about you?"

"It was a Monday." I take out the first black container. "What did you order?"

"Steak and salmon," he says as I take out another container. "I got two of each."

"There is enough food for six people," I say, and he just shrugs. I open the containers, and the smell makes my mouth water. "Beef or fish?" I look up at him.

"Steak," he says and I put steak on a plate with some roasted Brussel sprouts and a loaded baked potato. I walk over to him. "Here you go." I place the plate in front of him.

"Where is your plate?" he asks.

"I'm going to get some salmon and some salad." He looks over at me. "I just ran for two hours, you think I did that so I can eat carbs?" I turn to walk away and he grabs my arm, bringing me to him. His undoes the sash of my robe, his hand goes to my ass as he squeezes it.

"You're more than okay," he says and I look up at him. My mouth waters and it has nothing to do with the food waiting for me, no it's all this man. I shake my head, walking away as he slaps my ass.

I make my own plate opting, still for the salad and the grilled salmon. I sit next to him as we eat. "I leave tomorrow," he says from beside me, and I knew it was coming. "Team left today, and they play tomorrow."

"Do you always travel with the team?" I ask, and he nods his head.

"I don't really travel with the team, but I'm there for all their games. If they are travelling between games, depending on my schedule, I'll go with them or meet them there," he says, cutting into his steak.

"I leave in January for my tour," I say, grabbing some salad. "And I, for one, hate it."

"Your tour?" He looks over at me as I eat a piece of salmon.

"I go and meet the up and comings. See who I want to go after," I say and he just looks at me. "What?"

"You actually go to all the games?" I nod at him.

"I also meet the parents and get a feel for them. I also lay down the law," I say, picking up another piece.

"You law down the law," he repeats and I turn to him.

"My time is precious," I say, crossing my legs, the robe falling on both sides. "I want them to know what I can do for them. But I also want them to know what I'm not going to put up with."

He turns, pulling my chair closer to him as he opens his legs. "You work hard." I don't know if he's telling me or asking me. "I didn't call you today."

"I know," I say, not sure where this is going right now.

"It doesn't bother you." Again, I don't know if he is asking me or telling me.

"I know that you're busy," I say. "And I know that if you have a minute you will call me." I shrug. "Or maybe you won't, but it's not that big of a deal. I don't sit down and wait for your call if that is what you are asking." I smirk at him.

"I like you," he says the words that makes me stop breathing. He raises his hand and is rubbing my cheek with his thumb. "Like I really, really like you."

I laugh. "Well, if you are wondering, I like you, too," I admit to him.

"There are so many things that I like about you," he says, leaning in and kissing my lips. My hand comes out as I place my palm on his face. "But the thing I like most about you."

"Oh," I joke with him. "I know exactly what you like most about me."

He laughs. "I do really like that, but what I was going to say." He shakes his head. "Is that I don't have to apologize for who I am." I look at him, my eyebrows pinched together. "If I can't call you, you aren't going to hold a grudge. If I'm busy and can't see you, you aren't going to be pissed off."

"I didn't want to tell you this before," I say. "But now that we've shared our like for each other." Leaning in and kissing him. "I'm a great catch."

"That you are." He chuckles. "Now, finish eating so I can show you what else I like about you." My head goes back, and I laugh hysterically, my robe falling open, and he takes the opportunity to slip his hand in. "Are you done eating?" he asks, and with his hands on me, the last thing I think about is eating.

"I brought you coffee." I hear from the door the next morning while I run on the treadmill. I look at him dressed in his boxers and nothing else.

"You didn't have to get up," I say, slowly turning down the speed, coming down to a slight jog. "Did you sleep okay?" It's the first time he's slept over. It's the first time I've ever had anyone sleep over at my house, unless they were family members.

"Your bed smells of flowers," he says, sitting down on one of the chairs that I have in the gym area. "It smells like you."

"Is that a good thing or a bad thing?" I ask, stopping the treadmill and getting off.

Grabbing the towel and wiping my face, "It's a good thing." He smiles at me and tilts his head back for a kiss. "How long did you sleep?"

"If you left me alone after round three, it would have been longer." I kiss him. "I'll sleep well tonight."

"What time is your plane?" I ask, and he pulls me onto him. "I'm all sweaty," I say.

"I like you sweaty," he says, and I shake my head. "Let's get in the shower."

"One more for the road." I laugh with him and he picks me up, carries me back to my bedroom, and we both get to work later than was scheduled.

He doesn't call me that night but he does text me.

Nico: My bed smells like bleach.

I laugh and send him back a text.

Me: Better than wet socks

I think that he isn't going to answer me back, but he shocks me by calling me on FaceTime. "A text and a FaceTime," I joke with him. "I'm impressed, Mr. Edward."

He laughs and I see that he's lying in bed. "I missed your face," he says. "How was your day?"

"Uneventful. Same old. Little bit of small fires here and there but it made the day go a bit faster," I say. "The game was good."

"We should have won," he says. "But you can't win them all."

We talk for a bit longer and I hang up the phone and turn off the lights. I ignore the fact that I miss him. I ignore the fact that I didn't ask when he is going to be home and when my phone rings the next day and I look down hoping it's him, it's then I know that I'm in it more than I can admit.

"Hello," I say, seeing it's Manning.

"Hey there," he says and since he's left Murielle he's been happier than he has ever been. He's been even friendlier with the reporters. "Busy?"

"For you," I say to him. "Never."

"Good," he says. "Meet me in an hour." I look at my watch.

"It's five o'clock," I say.

"I know, we just landed," he says, and I lean back in my chair.

"The last time you asked me to meet you in an hour, your whole life exploded."

"I can assure you there is nothing wrong," he says, and I hear him honk his horn at something. "I'll text you the address."

"You owe me," I say and get up to go home, changing out of my skirt. Instead, I put on tight black pants with a loose silk shirt. I'm walking out of my building when the car gets here, and I get in.

I go on Instagram and see that Nico added a picture of the game last night. I try not to think about him getting in and not calling me. I don't have time because we pull up to the restaurant.

I walk in and see Manning sitting down at a table in the back with a woman beside him. He smiles when he sees me. "There she is."

"Here I am," I say when he gets up and comes to me, kissing me on the cheek.

"Becca," Manning says, looking over at the beautiful woman who has red hair and green eyes. "This is Evelyn."

My mouth opens as I finally meet the woman who gave life to this man again. "It's so great to finally meet you," Evelyn says. Getting up, she comes to me and gives me a hug. I get it now, why he feels for her. "I've heard all about the infamous Becca."

"Well, I don't know what he said," I say to her, smiling, "but if it's good, it's all true." She laughs and goes back to sit down in her seat. Manning sits next to her.

I sit in front of them. "I'm almost afraid to ask what this meeting is about." I put my hands on the table as the waiter comes over, and we order drinks. I turn back to them, a little nervous. "So tell me."

"I," Manning starts. "Actually, we wanted to take you out to thank you for everything that you did for us." I look at him as he puts his arms around Evelyn, and she looks up at him with hearts in her eyes. He kisses her lips. "I don't know how it would have gone down without your help."

"Well," I say, "after seeing the two of you together finally, I'm going to go out on a limb and say it was worth it."

"Sorry I'm late." I hear from beside me and look up, shocked to see Nico. He's wearing jeans and a sweater.

"No worries," Manning says, and I can only watch him.

It happens almost in slow motion. His head comes down, and he stops right before my lips. "Hey," he says right before he kisses my lips in front of everyone.

TWENTY-TWO

Nico

"HEY," I SAY right before kissing her lips. I hear a gasp coming from the other side of the table, and I know that there will be questions. I pull out the chair beside her and sit down, propping my arm around her shoulders.

I look over at her, and she, too, is in shock. I wish I could tell you that I had a plan, but I can't. When Manning told me he was going to take Becca out for dinner, I casually invited myself. He didn't think anything of it, and I can tell from everyone's face at the table that they have questions.

"Well." Manning is the first to speak. "This is." He puts up his hands and tries to find the words. Evelyn looks at him and then at Becca.

"This is great that you can join us," Evelyn says. "We owe you guys so much for all of your support, and I wish that we could explain to you guys exactly what it means to us." She looks over at Manning.

"Thanks for the invite," I say and rub her shoulder with my thumb. I missed her. It's fucking nuts, but I fucking missed her. I caved last night and texted her without trying to sound like a lovesick puppy. I was shocked she answered right away, my finger pressed the FaceTime before I thought out the game plan. Then her face filled the screen, and all the thoughts and plans were out the window. "Have you guys ordered yet?"

"No," Manning says, his eyes looking at me, asking me all the questions. I can feel Becca get stiff beside me. "I don't mean to be nosy. But when?"

"I guess it started at Candace's party and it's been slowly gaining speed," I say and look over at Becca, and her face tells me that she is not okay with any of this. But she puts on her poker face, and I can tell when she does it. A shield comes down. If you know her eyes, you can tell.

"Enough about us," she says, plastering a smile on her face. "How is everything going with you guys?"

Evelyn doesn't notice her change, but Manning does, and I know that he's going to let me off the hook for Evelyn's sake, but he is going to have words for me later. "Things are actually calming down." She looks over at Manning, and her smile gets even bigger. "It's almost as if it's yesterday's news."

"There is always a bigger story," Becca says. "Big news today, cat litter news tomorrow."

"I've never heard that saying," I say from beside her, and she doesn't turn to look at me.

"I was mostly worried for Jaxon," Evelyn says and

you can see tears coming to her eyes as she blinks them away. "I didn't want him to feel any of the negative that was coming our way."

"Well, at least one of us cared about that," Manning says. "Murielle was more than okay spilling the beans to him that Evelyn and I were a couple." He puts his hand on hers, she turns it over and their hands link. I look at them and I have the sudden need to hold Becca's hand. I sit back watching how they act, and it scares me when I finally realize that this is how I feel about Becca. I mean we haven't said the words out loud yet, but I love spending time with her. I love when we talk, and I love when we don't talk and all we do is sit there in our own little world, but knowing we are just next to each other comforts me in a way I didn't know existed.

The meal goes off with the subject staying light. Becca is still acting the part, and I hate it. When we get up to leave, I grab her hand, and I'm surprised she lets me, to be honest. We walk out, and she hugs Manning and then Evelyn, thanking them for a lovely dinner.

"Where are you parked?" She looks at me and asks, and I just point at the SUV.

She walks with me. "Becca." I say her name, and she turns around.

"No," she says, looking around again to make sure that no one is looking our way. "We are not doing this in the middle of a fucking public parking lot where people can hear us, or better yet take a picture of us." She opens the SUV door and gets in. I walk around the SUV and get into it, making my way to her place since it's closer.

The doorman comes to the door, opening it for her. I get out, grabbing my bag and walk in with her. She can be mad all she wants. I'm not leaving here tonight. Her eyes go to the bag, and she doesn't say anything either.

She walks ahead of me to her bedroom once we get into her place. I place the bag on the bed and then turn to her, but she doesn't wait another second. "What the fuck was that?" she asks, pointing at the door.

"What was what?" I pretend not to know what she's talking about, but I know exactly what she means.

"Don't do that." She folds her arms. "You kissed me."

"I've kissed you many times before," I point out, taking off my jacket, assuming she isn't going to kick me out on my ass. I toss the jacket on the chair in the corner.

"You kissed me in the middle of a public restaurant with eyes on us," she says, and I wait for her to finish. "You kissed me in front of Manning."

"Okay." I take off my cuff links, walking over to the bedside table and placing them on there.

"Nico," she says my name. "We haven't even discussed what this is." She points at me and then to her. "This whole thing." Her hand goes in a circle. "Whatever this is."

"I thought we spoke about it," I say, and she glares at me. "I told you I like you."

"Well, I like Manning," she says, and it's time for me to glare. "You don't see me kissing his lips."

"That's not funny." I put my hands on my hips.

"I'm not trying to be funny." She mimics my stance.

"What do you think this is?" I ask, and she tilts her

head.

"I have no idea what it is," she answers right away. "I was not putting a label on it. I thought we were friends with perks."

I glare at her, and she doesn't finish her sentence. "Do you have any other friends with—"

"I suggest you think about that question before you say it out loud," she warns. "What is this?"

"It's a man and a woman who enjoy spending their time together," I say, and it sounds stupid even to my ears. She rolls her eyes. "Okay, fine."

"You kissed me in front of a lot of people," she says softly. "You kissed me in front of Manning. It's my work, and I have a reputation."

"I know," I say softly, and I go to her. "But I'm not sorry about it."

"That doesn't answer my question, Nico," she says. "You didn't even talk to me about it."

"That's because it happened so fast. I didn't expect it to. I walked into the restaurant, knowing I was going to see you. What I wasn't expecting is how it would feel seeing you after two days. Then I walked in," I say, "I saw you, and I missed you. I didn't think about anything but kissing you." I put my hands on her hips. "But you're right. I should have spoken to you about it. We should have had the conversation."

She steps out of my reach. "You are right. We should have a discussion about this."

"Perfect." I put my hands in my pockets. "Why don't you start?"

"What are we going to tell people?" she asks, and I just look at her.

"I don't usually have to answer to anyone." She tilts her head to the side. "I don't."

"That makes two of us. But that you kissed me in a room full of people, so the rules have changed." Fuck, if I didn't think she was hot before, the no-nonsense Becca makes me even harder.

"So we are dating," I finally say.

"Exclusively?" she asks, and I glare at her. "It's a valid question. We haven't had a talk about our past."

"Considering it is in the past, I don't see why we even have to discuss that part," I say. "Are you saying you haven't been exclusive up to now?" She glares at me, and the thought of her with someone else makes my blood boil.

"I'm not even going to justify answering that. So we got that part checked off. Let's discuss the dating part." I wait for her to start. "Phone calls."

"At least one a day," I say, and she raises her eyebrow. "I like talking to you before bed," I admit to her.

"So do I," she says softly. "So at least once a day."

"I know we both work like crazy." I'm the one who talks next. "But I think making time for each other has to be a must."

"I agree," she says. "Lies. I won't put up with them." I nod. "We are both grown ass adults. If we have to lie to each other, it defeats the purpose of us even dating. If at any time it's not working for one of us, tell the other."

"Sleepovers." I get to the good stuff.

"What about them?" she asks, smirking.

"I want them," I say. "If I'm home and you're home, I want us to be together."

"I can do that," she says, and I just look at her. "Fine." She throws up her hands. "I want us to be together also."

"So I think we've covered everything," I say.

"I have to tell my brothers," she says. "It's only fair."

"I'll tell Lizzie." I look down. "She kind of already knows, but I'll confirm it."

"The press?" she asks. "Not that it's any of their business, but if they get whiff of this?"

"So how about we tell our inner circle first and see how it goes, and then when we are both ready, we can make it official publicly?" She nods her head. "But I'm not going to not kiss you if we are in public. I refuse to do that. If I want to kiss you, I'm going to kiss you. I'm not a fucking teenager who has to hide from their parents."

"Well, then I think we got it all settled," she says, coming to me. "I also believe we just had our first fight." I look at her, confused when she puts her hands around my neck. "And from what I've heard, make-up sex is better than regular sex."

I throw my head back and laugh. "Sex with you is out of this world to begin with."

"Smooth." She kisses my lips. "Very smooth." I pick her up, and she wraps her legs around my waist.

"I'd like to add something to the agenda," I say, walking toward her bed. "Skirts. I like you in skirts."

"What, why?" she asks me.

"Easy access, baby," I say, my head going to the side, and my mouth opening to hers. I rip off her pants, and she was right. Make-up sex trumps all the sex I've ever had in my life.

TWENTY-THREE

BECCA

ME: I NEED to speak to both of you tomorrow. Let me know when is good for you guys.

I put down the phone and look up when I hear Nico walking back into the room. "Who are you on the phone with?" he asks, and I look at him, my mouth watering as I take him in. He is wearing a white towel around his waist, and it falls just a bit low, showing you his V. Another white towel is in his hand as he dries the water from his hair.

"I was telling my other guys that I'm exclusive now." I wink at him. He stops wiping his hair and glares at me. "Too soon?" I ask, and he drops the towel from his hand.

"Why are you dressed?" he asks, his eyes roaming over my tank top and panties.

"Naked," he says one word. "Always naked in bed."

"Is this part of the agreement?" I ask and just look at him. When he came into the restaurant, I was shocked but excited to see him, then my happiness in seeing him went out the window when he kissed me. I was shocked that he would just put it out there, and then I was angry that he did it without taking into account how I felt. The minute it happened, I heard Manning gasp out loud and knew he would have questions.

"I just added it," he says, dropping the towel around his waist. "So naked."

My eyes go to his cock that is slowly waking up for a round two, or actually round three if you count the shower. "What are we going to tell everyone who asks about when this started?"

"The truth," he says, getting into the bed under the covers. He comes over to me and wraps his arms around my waist. "Now why do you still have clothes on?" His hand goes to my breast as he pulls down the strap and takes one nipple in his mouth.

"I can't concentrate when your mouth is on me," I say, my eyes looking down while he pushes the other side down and the straps snap. "You just ruined my tank top."

"Hmm …" he moans, biting down on my nipple. "That's your fault."

"Really?" I say, and he takes his time showing me why it's best for me to go to bed naked.

"I CAN GET used to this," I say when he comes into the room, holding a cup of coffee for me.

"Well, I aim to please," he says, sitting in the chair and looking up at the television. "She is a firecracker in bed, and she watches sports news in the morning," he says, bringing the cup to his lips. "You're right, you are a great catch."

I shake my head and continue my run while he watches the television. "One of these days, I'm going to fuck you on your treadmill," he says once I stop running and I'm drinking water. I suddenly choke and start coughing. "If you think your ass looks good in a dress, you should see that bounce when you run."

"Good to know you approve," I say, trying to catch my breath. He groans, his hand covering his cock.

"Actually, if you bend over right now." He gets up, coming to me. "I can see if your ass can bounce like that when I slam into you."

My mouth hangs open. "I'm sweaty." I look down at myself. "And not just the little sweat from sex," I say. He leans into me, and I duck out of the way. "No." I shake my head. "We can see if my ass bounces tonight."

"We can try in the shower," he says, slapping my ass as we walk back to my bedroom. He walks over to the bedside table and takes out two condoms.

"Um, why the two?" I ask, and he winks at me.

"One for the shower," he says, holding up his finger. "And one for when I bend you over when you do your makeup." It's a good thing I am holding on to said counter or my knees would go weak.

"We need to get our timing more in sync," I say, coming out of my walk-in closet and seeing him put on his button-down shirt. His hair still wet from the shower that he just got out of.

"What does that mean?" he asks as he tucks his shirt in.

"It means that I usually leave home at eight thirty, and it's nine fifteen. So if we are going to do two rounds in the morning, we need to get our timing right."

He smirks at me. "Negative."

"We should discuss it," I say, and he looks me up and down. I'm wearing a white tight skirt with black trim and a slit on the right side.

"When you get that look." I point at him. "There is no discussion. It's more of a pounce."

He laughs. "I'm not going to go faster." He sits on the bed, putting on his shoes.

"What if we do it once instead of twice?" I sit next to him, slipping on my black patent heels.

"Negative," he says, leaning to me and kissing my neck.

"So no discussion then." I walk to grab my purse, turning, and I'm surprised he's right behind me.

"Your ass looks good in that skirt," he says, and I laugh at him, pushing him away.

"My ass always looks good to you," I say, and his phone rings. "Now go to work."

"Give me a kiss," he says, smirking, and I lean my head back as his tongue slides into my mouth. His kisses leave me breathless, and right before I'm about to take him back to bed, his phone rings again. "Have a nice day."

"I will," I say and turn to walk out of my bedroom. "Call me later." He walks out of my bedroom now. "What are you doing?"

"Thinking of all the ways I'm going to use that ass tonight." He smirks and puts the phone to his ear, not giving me a chance to answer him.

I walk into the office thirty minutes later with a coffee in my hand. "Good morning, Erika."

She looks up from her computer. "Good morning." She smiles at me. "You have a package."

I look in my office, seeing the huge bouquet of red roses sitting in the middle of my desk. I walk in and grab the white card, taking it out.

Roses are red.

Red is the color of sex.

That is all I got.

N

I throw my head back and laugh, grabbing my phone and calling him. He answers after two rings. "Well, this is a nice surprise."

"What do you mean?" I ask, surprised.

"Did you notice that you've never called me?" he points out, and I sit down.

"I have, too."

"Not really since we got together," he says, and I hear a car door close.

"I'm going to have to check and get back to you about that," I say, and he laughs. "But the reason I was calling is to thank you for the flowers."

"You're welcome." He connects to the Bluetooth.

"I didn't know you were a poet," I joke with him, leaning back in my chair. "You learn something new every day." I look over and see Francis standing there. "I have to run. I'll talk to you later." I disconnect and put the phone down. "It's rude to eavesdrop."

"I wasn't eavesdropping. I was being polite and not interrupting you." He comes into my office. "Are those from who I think they are from?" I don't have time to answer his question because Trevor comes into the office.

"Glad you could join us." He looks at me, and my eyebrows pinch together.

"Are you talking to me?" I ask, confused by his comment.

He nods his head. "You just got in, and it's almost noon." I roll my eyes.

"It's just past ten." I point at him. "The office opens at nine."

"Which still makes you late." He shrugs and sits down in the chair beside Francis. "Now what is this meeting about?"

I get up and walk over to the door, closing it, turning just in time to see Trevor and Francis share a look. "I texted you guys," I say, and I don't know why I'm suddenly nervous. Well, I kind of know why I'm nervous because I really like Nico, and if my brothers say anything bad about him, I might have to kick them in the balls. "Because I wanted to give you a heads-up."

"You're pregnant," Francis says first, and I glare at him.

"Very funny." I look at both of them. "I'm dating

Nico Harrison."

"What do you mean by you're dating Nico?" Francis asks.

"You need to clarify that just a touch more," Trevor says,

"It's pretty fucking self-explanatory," I say. "I'm dating him."

They just look at me. "We are in a relationship."

"Shut the fuck up." Francis is the first to say anything. "Is this an exclusive thing, or do you guys go out, hook-up, and then maybe hook-up again?"

"Have you ever looked up the meaning of a relationship before?" Trevor looks over at him. "How long has this been going on?"

"We came out publicly yesterday," I say. "We've been together a while."

"Does that mean the press got a hold of the story, and you want us to say no comment?" Trevor just looks at me.

"No," I say. "I'm saying we had dinner yesterday, and he kissed me in front of people. I didn't want you guys to hear it from anyone but me."

"You know that this is a horrible, horrible idea," Trevor says. I glare at him, and he knows, so he just holds up his hand. "I'm not saying he's a bad guy. I'm just saying that I don't think this is your best idea."

"Give her a break, will you." Francis looks over at Trevor. "It's Becca. She wouldn't just jump into shit without thinking about it."

"That's right," I agree with Francis. "But to answer

your question. I don't think this is a horrible idea." It hurts to even think that it is. "It's a guy and a girl enjoying each other's company."

"It's not a merger," Francis says. "You don't have to be all technical and shit. Just say I like him."

"Fine," I huff out. "I like him." I look at both of them. "A lot."

"How do you think other people will feel about this?" Trevor asks.

"It has nothing to do with anyone but us." I sit up straight.

"People might think you give him special treatment," Francis points out.

"That is the furthest from the truth," I tell them.

"I know that, and you know that," Trevor says. "But all of them." He points at the office. "They don't know that."

"Well, then that's a them problem. I'm not going to let people dictate who I can and can't date." I look at them. "Also, this isn't up for discussion. I didn't ask you to come in here to get your approval." They just look at me. "I asked you to come in here so you don't get blindsided in case someone sees us." I don't leave room for them to say anything.

"Thank you," Trevor says, getting up. "Also, off the record, if he hurts you, he is going to kick his ass." I laugh.

"You don't get your hands dirty," I point out.

"I didn't say I was going to kick his ass." He laughs. "I'm going to send Francis after him."

"I have been hitting the weights pretty hard lately," he says, getting up and walking out of the office after Trevor.

My phone pings with a text.

Nico: Might be late tonight. I'll know more later.

TWENTY-FOUR

Nico

CHECKING MY SCHEDULE once I get in, I see I have a meeting with the events people to discuss the coming months activities. I put my phone down as soon as I send the text to Becca. My eyes never leave the screen with her reply, a smile filling my face.

Becca: Thank you for the flowers. Let me know later.

The sound of someone knocking on my door makes me look up. "Hey," Lizzie says, coming in and closing the door. "So."

"So what?" I say, my heart beating a million miles a minute. I close my eyes, the throbbing starting to pound in my temples.

"What are you going to do?" she asks, sitting down in front of my desk in one of the empty seats.

"I have no fucking idea," I say, my chest getting tighter and tighter. I just had a meeting with Laurene. "I guess

I have no fucking choice at this point."

She looks at me. "She would do it for you without thinking twice."

"I know that," I say. "One hundred percent know that if the roles were reversed, she wouldn't even think twice about it."

"I don't get it then," she says to me. "What's the problem then?"

"It's just …" I say, but I don't know what to say really. I don't know how it happened or when it happened, but Becca has crept her way into my bones. Everything about her makes my chest fill up and my face break into a smile. But not just any smile, the kind of smile that hurts your face. I look at my phone again, and just seeing her name makes my stomach sink. "It's just bad timing."

"Is there ever a right time for this?" Lizzie asks. I want to stand and throw something against the fucking wall. I want to yell at the top of my lungs.

"Yes, actually," I say, my voice coming out pissed off. "There is a fucking time for this, and it was a month ago or even two months ago." Basically, it was before Becca was in the picture.

She just looks at me, and I know she is trying to help, but right now, it isn't helping. Nothing is helping by knowing that. I stand, going over to the window and look out. The dread just sinking into me. "I'm sure," Lizzie says, and I shake my head.

"Don't," I say, and a knock on the door has Lizzie getting up. I don't have time to sit and think of a solution because something else comes up, and by the time I look out, it's close to seven.

Lizzie pokes her head in. "Are you heading out?" she asks, and I nod my head. "See you tomorrow morning. The plane is leaving at eight."

My stomach sinks again, but nothing can prepare me for the way it hurts when my phone rings, and I see it's Becca.

"Hey," I say, putting the phone to my ear.

"Well, hello there," she says, and the smile comes automatically. "Are you still at work?"

"Technically, yes," I say, pressing the elevator button. "But I'm on my way home now."

"Did you want to get dinner?" she asks. "I can pick something up, or we can not." She sounds nervous.

"How about you meet me at my place?" I say, getting into my SUV. "I have meals delivered, and if not, we can get something ordered."

"Are you sure?" she asks, and her voice goes low. "It's fine either way. I've had a long day anyway."

"I'll send you the address. Go there now. If you get there before me, I can give you the code for the gate." She laughs. "It's twenty-five twenty-six. For next time or this time or whenever you want to stop by."

"I'll see you soon." She hangs up, and I forward her my address. She replies that she is twenty minutes away.

We get there at the same time. I walk over to her, wrapping my arm around her waist. "Hi," I whisper right before my mouth claims hers. My tongue mixes with hers, and I don't want to let her go. She molds into me and wraps one arm around my neck and the other goes to my chest.

"Hi," she says when I finally release her. I turn, putting one hand around her shoulder as we walk up the steps to go into the house. "How was your day?"

"Good," I lie. "Long. What about you?" I ask when we walk into the house. My arm never leaves her shoulder. She sets her purse down on the table in the middle of the foyer. I slip off my jacket and toss it on the table next to her purse. I stand here for a second, looking at her stuff mixed with mine.

"It was good. The same." My hand reaches out, linking my fingers with hers. "I told my brothers about us," she says, and I look down at the floor, not ready to look up yet. The heaviness in my heart gets stronger and stronger.

"What did they say?" I ask, looking over at her and then looking away as fast as I looked at her. The pain is too much to look at her right now.

"Normal stuff I guess," she says as we walk into the kitchen. I let her hand go to go to the fridge. "Obviously, they weren't happy-ish with the news." I look over at her and see her eyes down, looking at her fingers in front of her. "But it's not their decision. It's mine."

The lump in my throat forms, and all I can do is nod. I fucking nod. I grab two meals, not knowing what it is and just pop them into the microwave. "Are you okay to eat out of the container, or do you want to plate it?"

"I'm good with the container," she says, pulling out one of the stools at the island counter. "This kitchen is huge," she says, and I turn to the sound of the microwave beeping. I check and add more time.

"Do you want something to drink?" I ask, going to the fridge and seeing if there is an open bottle of white wine. "I have wine, beer, soda."

"I'll have water," she says, and I hear the sound of her shoes coming closer to me. "Do you want me to get the forks and knives?" she asks from beside me. I look over at her, and my heart speeds up because she takes my breath away when she looks at me. Her eyes light as she comes closer to me. I tilt my head down a bit, and she leans in and kisses me.

"Let's eat," I say when the microwave beeps. I sit next to her, not even caring what I'm eating. I don't think I taste anything.

"Do you have a busy day tomorrow?" she asks, and I nod.

"I have a flight at eight," I say. "Then I have a meeting before the hockey game."

"How long are you gone for?" she asks, and I shrug while I chew.

"I think two days," I say. "I didn't really check." I take the phone out of my pocket and check. "Yeah, I'm back in two days."

The rest of dinner is awkward, or at least, I think it's awkward. "I think I'm going to head out," she says when I close the dishwasher, and I look over at her.

"What?" I ask, shocked. "Why?"

"Well," she says, looking down, "you seem like something is on your mind." I want to kick myself for making her feel uncomfortable. "I don't want to bother you." She smiles, but I can see that her eyes have darkened a bit. I walk to her and put my hands on her face.

My thumbs rub her cheeks. "Stay," I say softly, her hands going to my waist. "Please."

She looks down and then up again. "If at anytime you want me to leave or things just get overwhelming, it's okay to want alone time." She smirks. "Trust me, I get it."

"You mean that, don't you?" I don't know why I'm shocked about her being even more awesome than I thought she was.

"Well, yeah," she says, rolling her eyes. "Sometimes we have a day when we just want to go home, sit on the couch, and destroy a whole pint of ice cream." She laughs, and I put my lips on hers.

"I want you to stay." We walk up the stairs without saying anything. We walk into my bedroom, and I turn on the soft lights and pull her to me. The kiss is soft and slow. Her hand goes to my shirt, untucking it from my pants. My hand goes to her waist, taking out the black tight shirt I saw her put on this morning. I pull it over her head, our mouths separating only for a second until her shirt is off. I feel her fingers slowly move their way down my shirt, one button at a time.

We take our time undressing each other, our hands and mouth always touching. When I lay her down in the middle of my bed, my kisses linger from her mouth to her neck, slowly sucking in. I make my way down to one nipple. Sucking it deep into my throat and taking the other one. I spend my time making sure that I kiss every single inch of her.

I make her come twice before she turns, then sits up and pulls me up to kiss my mouth. "Sit," she says, and I turn, sitting in the middle of the bed with my back to the headboard. She takes my cock in her hand and slowly slides her mouth down it. I move her hair to the other side so I can see her face. I want to watch her all night long. She works me over and over and when I come, I whisper her name.

Rolling over to the side, I grab a condom and slide it down my cock. She puts her leg over my hips and then slides down. Neither of us says anything, and it's the strangest thing. It's almost as if she knows I can't talk. It's almost as if she knows I need her to just be here. The only sound in the room right now is our heavy breathing.

She wraps her arms around my neck, and my hand wraps around her waist while the other reaches up her back to grab her neck. I bury my face in her neck as she throws her head back. She moves up and down. I don't push her and let her lead the whole way.

The whole night, I don't sleep. I just watch her, reaching out to touch and hold her and silently tell her how I feel about her. I get up right before I know her alarm is going to go off and set it for later.

I get dressed, picking up my bag and walking over to her. She still sleeps, the white shirt at her neck, one arm out and the other around her waist. I lean forward, kissing her softly and hoping she wakes up, but she doesn't. I'm not surprised since I barely let her sleep last night.

I grab a paper and leave her a note telling that I'll

call her later. I put it right on top of her phone. I know I should turn around and walk out, but I don't. I take one more look at her and give her one more kiss. Then I walk out, hoping like fuck I can survive this.

TWENTY-FIVE

Becca

My eyes slowly open, and I see the sun coming in. Turning my head to the side, I see that I'm all alone. "Nico?" I say his name, sitting up and looking to see that it's past eight thirty in the morning. "Fuck," I say, grabbing my phone. The white note on top slips to the floor. I pick it up and see his writing.

Turned off your alarm. You worked out enough last night. I'll call you later.

N

I get out of bed and call Erika first. "Good morning," she answers, and I know she's at her desk.

"Sorry, I had an early call this morning," I lie, walking over to my clothes in the middle of the bedroom. "I'll be in a bit later."

"No worries," she says, and I get dressed. I walk over and fix his bed, not knowing if he has a cleaning lady coming in or not.

I walk out of the house, trying not to think about last night too much. It was a quiet one. I know he had something on his mind because I felt it the whole way during dinner.

I felt it every single time he reached for me, but I gave him whatever he wanted. I make it to my house and get into the shower, then decide I'm going to just work from home. The day is slow and quiet, and when I go to bed, it's without a word or a text from him. I wake up a couple of times during the night and check my phone to see if he called. There is nothing there, not even a text, so I end up tossing and turning most of the night.

When my alarm rings the next day, I reach over and turn it off. I slip into my gym stuff, grabbing a bottle of water on my way to the gym. I get on the treadmill, taking the remote out.

I press the power button as the sound fills the room. *SportsCenter* shows the highlights of the game last night. They start talking about the game and how they won in overtime. A screen shot shows Nico putting his hand in a fist, celebrating when they win. I smile, thinking about how much I miss seeing him.

Then it happens so quickly I don't know it's actually happening.

"Well, the Oilers won the game on the same night their owner secretly got married." I almost fall and smash my face when my head snaps back so fast. The sound of the remote falling out of my hand and onto the treadmill smashing into the wall behind me. It's the same sound my heart makes.

This is not happening. My heart starts to beat so fast it echoes in my ears like a herd of bulls charging down the streets of Spain. I rewind the show and listen to it again. The words replay over and over again as I run out of my exercise room toward my computer in my home office. It takes a minute to open, but in that time, I feel like I'm going to throw up. I start pacing back and forth and when the screen saver comes on, my hands shake so bad I can't type in the words that I'm going to google.

Nico Harrison is married. I press enter, the first search coming up is Page Six news.

I scan the headlines: **Dallas Oilers Owner and Most Eligible Bachelor is no more. Nico Harrison marries oil heiress Laurene Christy.**

My knees give out, and I fall to the floor, my hands stopping my face from smashing into the floor. I have just enough time to grab the garbage can before I throw up.

My phone rings from somewhere in the house. I wipe my mouth with the back of my hand. Getting up, I don't even notice the tears on my face. I don't notice until the sob rips through me, and I have to hold onto the wall as I walk to my bedroom. The phone rings again and again, but my eyes and feet are too scared to move in its direction. I feel the room spinning around me, or maybe it's my head that is spinning.

Along with the phone ringing, I hear my front door open. I look in shock and afraid in case it's Nico. The echoing sound of my breath fills my ears. I don't know if I should run or stay. I'm like a deer caught in the headlights when I see it's Francis. He stands there in shorts and a T-shirt. I hated it when he bought a condo in my building, but I'm thankful for it right now. "So I take it you heard the news."

I don't say anything. Instead, a sob comes out of me. My hand flies to my mouth to stop it from escaping, but I'm not fast enough. My body starts to shake uncontrollably. I feel like I'm falling, but I don't crash into the floor this time. Instead, Francis is catching me. He's picking me up off my feet. "That motherfucker," he hisses as my phone rings again.

He looks at me as I bury my face in my hands. "This can't be happening," I say in a whisper. "It can't be."

I look at Francis, whose phone rings. He picks it up. "Yeah, I'm with her now." He looks at me. "It's Trevor," he says and then listens to what Trevor says. "How the fuck should I know?" he yells. "From the looks of her, she didn't know anything."

I reach for my phone, seeing the missed calls. Twenty-three calls from Nico. All this morning along with voice mails.

My hands shake, and I get up on auto pilot. I walk to my closet, taking down a bag. "What are you doing?" Francis asks.

"What does it look like I'm doing?" I say, wiping tears away with the back of my hand.

"It looks like you're running away." He baits me and I shake my head.

"I guess you can say I'm running away." I start putting things in the bag. "I have a couple of kids I need to go and meet," I say, not even sure I know what I'm packing. I'm just throwing shit in my bag.

"That's a good idea," he says, his phone beeping again. "Did you know?"

"Are you kidding me, Francis?" I hiss at him. "Do you think I'd be involved with him? I was with him two days ago."

"He didn't tell you?" he asks again.

"Francis." I say his name, and he holds up his hands. "I think I would remember him saying, 'Oh, hey, Becca, come over to eat dinner because I'm getting married tomorrow.'"

"Are you going to talk to him?" he asks, and I stand here with my heart shattered in my chest. Literally, it feels like I'm walking on shards of glass with no shoes on.

"I don't think there is anything that I can say to him," I answer, and the pain rips through me again. My hand goes to my chest to stop the pressure. "I have nothing to say to him."

"I mean, there are always three sides to a story," he says, and I zip the bag closed.

"Pretty sure there are not three sides to someone getting married," I say the words. I walk over to my phone and call Erika, who answers right away.

"Becca." She says my name, and I hate that people are feeling bad for me. I close my eyes to stop the tears from coming, but they come anyway.

"Hey." I try to talk without it sounding like I have a frog in my throat. "I need you to get me a private plane in the next hour," I say.

"Where are we going?" she asks, and I know that she is going to be on the plane with me.

"I have a couple of kids in New York I want to see. Then I think we should head to Chicago," I say. "Let's start with New York and work from there."

"I'll get you a room at—" I stop her from talking.

"I want another hotel," I say right away.

"I'll fix it and send you the details for the plane," she says, and I hang up the phone.

"You know he's going to come looking for you," Francis says, and I sit on my bed. My hands still tremble a bit when I see that he's texted me.

"Why?" I don't know what exactly I'm asking him. It's a loaded question. Why did he do this? Why didn't I see it? Why did I fall for him? Why did he break my heart?

"I don't know him well," he says, looking at me, "but something tells me he's not going to stop until you hear him out."

"Well." I get up, looking at him. "You make sure when he does come around looking for me." I pull my shoulders back. "Which I don't think he will. But give him a message, will you? Tell him the contract is null and void."

"Are you sure you really want me to give him a message?" he asks, crossing his arms over his chest. "I'm not feeling friendly."

"Well, tell him or don't tell him," I say as my phone pings. "Now, I have a plane to catch."

"How pissed are you right now?" he asks, and I look at him.

"I'm beyond pissed," I say. "But you should know that I loved him." I don't change it to I love him because I want to pretend I don't. "So I'm more heartbroken than I've ever been. With that said, I'll be fine."

"Oh, I know you will," he says. "I'm going to go and get dressed, and I'll drive you to the plane."

"No," I say, shaking my head. "Erika already got me a car." I stay strong until I hear the front door slam shut. I walk to the shower, and only when I'm in the shower do the sobs rip through me. I sink to the floor, my eyes closing, and all I can see is his face. His smile, his smirk, his frown, his glare. Him.

I force myself to get up and get dressed. I force myself not to check anymore articles. I force myself to smile at the doorman who helps me with my luggage. I force myself to pretend everything is okay.

I pretend that it's just another day, except this time it's not. Erika is waiting for me with worry all over her face when she looks up from her phone. "Sorry for keeping you," I say, walking to the plane with her behind me. "Good morning," I say to the attendant waiting for us.

"We will be off in ten minutes," Erika says from behind me, and I sit in the chair.

My phone rings again in my pocket, and I take it out, seeing his name. The lump in my throat creeps up. I decline the call, and a minute later, I get a notification that I have a voice mail. I pick up my phone with a tear leaking out of one eye. I use my thumb to catch it as I grab my bag and take out my sunglasses.

I press the voice mail tab and see that they are all from him. I click edit in the corner and slowly click on every single one. Once they are all checked, my finger goes to the delete button. With a shaky hand, I press delete, then set my phone down.

With my heart pounding in my chest, my stomach burning, and my body shaking, I see the text that appears on the screen.

*Nico: **You need to call me, Becca.***
*Nico: **Please, Becca.***
*Nico: **I'm so sorry.***

TWENTY-SIX

Nico

I DIAL HER number again, hoping to God she just picks up the phone. When she doesn't, I pitch my phone at the wall. "Fuck!" I roar out, putting my hands into my hair and pulling it. *This is not happening, this is not happening*, I repeat over and over again.

Lizzie walks into the room, wearing her pjs and a robe, pushing a room service cart. "Add get new phone to my list," she says and I look at her. She woke me up two hours ago when the story broke. I knew right away it wasn't good when she pounded on my door.

I'm dressed in the same thing I wore last night. I went to bed with the biggest headache of my life, and all I wanted was to call Becca, but I couldn't. The fear crept into me, and I decided I would tell her everything in the morning. Only the world beat me to it.

"How bad is it?" I ask. She looks over at me and sits on the couch in the hotel room.

"It's everywhere." She looks down and then looks up. "We've gotten calls from everyone, and I mean everyone. They want an exclusive."

I walk over to look out the window as my heart sinks. "How the fuck did this happen?" I snap at the same time a knock sounds on the door.

Lizzie gets up, walking to the door. She opens the door, and Laurene walks in. "What the hell is going on?" she asks, standing there in the same outfit that Lizzie wears.

"What the hell is going on?" I shout back at her, and she looks at Lizzie, unsure if she should say anything or not. "What the hell is going on?" My voice gets louder. "My whole life is in fucking ruin."

"Can he be more dramatic?" Laurene says, looking at Lizzie who just shakes her head. Laurene looks at me, then back at Lizzie. "I need coffee," she says, walking over to the cart without a worry in the world, yet my life is in shatters. She takes a sip of her coffee. "Now can you calm down and tell me what is going on?"

"You obviously haven't heard the news, or seen the papers or even looked at your phone!" I shout, and I'm waiting for someone to contact the front desk about my yelling at five in the morning. I'm always in control and the fact that this is not in my control is over the top. I try not to think of the fact that I can't talk to Becca because that just enrages me more than anything.

"I didn't look at anything. It's five in the morning," she says, folding her arms over her chest, and I want to shake her.

"Well, I'll fill you in then." I walk over to her. "The press knows." Her eyes go wide as she looks from me to Lizzie.

"No." She shakes her head. "That's impossible. We had everyone sign an NDA." Her eyes go big. "You're lying."

"Do you think I would be up at five in the morning raging if I was lying?" I look at her.

She sets her coffee cup down. "We made sure that we went in there separately." She mentions of going to the lawyer's office. "Everything was done with extreme caution."

"Okay," Lizzie says, sitting down next to Laurene. "I hate to point it out that you two are well known," she says, then looks straight at me. "You are the most eligible bachelor. Did you not think that your name would ping somewhere?" I glare at her. "It could have been anyone who saw the paper and cashed in on it."

"So what do we do now?" Laurene asks.

"There is nothing to do now," Lizzie says, her eyes still watching me. "You can't come out and say it's fake." She's almost reading my mind.

"Fuck no," Laurene says, getting up. "We did all this for a reason."

"Laurene." I say her name, and she looks at me.

"No." She points at me. "I am so close. You prom-ised."

"When I was fucking eighteen!" I shout back at her.

"I would do it for you without thinking twice!" she yells, and I know she would. "I know this isn't what we thought was going to happen.”

“It was supposed to be ninety days and that’s it.” I rub my temples. “That is what you said. Ninety days and then we annul it.”

“It’s been one day.” She puts up one finger. “Eighty-nine more to go.”

“I need to go home.” I look at Lizzie, and she nods, getting up and grabbing her phone.

“Maybe once you’re home, you’ll calm down,” Laurene says, getting up and grabbing her coffee.

“Debatable,” Lizzie mumbles, not looking up as her fingers go nuts on her phone.

“What are we going to say to the press?” Laurene asks me.

“Nothing. Not a word. Not a comment. Nothing,” I say, not adding to the fact I’m not saying anything to anyone until I speak with Becca. Just the thought that she found out without me telling her puts pressure on my chest. I sit down and put my elbows on my knees, my head falling forward. I can’t even imagine what is going through her mind. I can’t even imagine how much it hurt her. The pressure on my chest is like an elephant sitting down right in the middle of it.

“You know if you say nothing, it will just target you more,” Lizzie says, and I swear I don’t think I’ve ever felt more defeated in my life. “They are going to hound the both of you.”

“She’s right,” Laurene says.

“I’m not saying a fucking word to the press right now.” I get up and look at Lizzie. “Not a fucking word.

Not from us, not from the organization, not from the fucking queen of England. Nothing." I get up. "You either." I point at Laurene. "Not a word."

"Lizzie is right," she says. "We should at least put out a joint statement."

"We are not saying anything yet," I say. "Nothing. I need to get home and …" I don't say another word. I just go into the room and pack my shit.

I take my shit and toss it into the bag. My head is swimming, and I suddenly feel like I'm drowning. I reach for my phone, and I come up empty, so all I can do is sit on the bed. I wonder where she is and who she is with. If she believes any of it.

There is a knock on the door, and I look up. "Hey," Lizzie says, poking her head in.

"Your phone is shattered, so I put the SIM card in this one." She hands me the phone. "I thought that you might want it."

"She isn't going to answer me." My voice is low, and Lizzie comes over and sits next to me. "Fuck." I shake my head. "I wouldn't talk to me."

"I'm sure once you tell her everything," Lizzie says quietly.

I take the phone and text Manning and Miller the same text.

Me: Call me when you get this text.

I then call her again, and it goes straight to voice mail this time. I hear her voice, and the pressure that I felt before comes back. I have to rub my chest. "We can leave. The plane is waiting," Lizzie tells me, and I nod at her. "I know that you are going through something right now." I look up at her, and I wonder if she can see what I'm going through.

"She is never going to talk to me again." I say the words I've been afraid to think since I first opened my eyes, and my nightmare started. "With all of this." I shake my head, and I feel the sting coming to my eyes. "She'll never talk to me again."

"She's a smart woman," Lizzie says, and I want to tell her that she is more than that. She's smart, she's funny, she's beautiful, and she's the most loyal person I've ever met. "But." I look over at her, not sure I want to hear the but. "But if you don't give the press anything, they are going to hound you even more, and it's not going to be good for anyone."

"I'm not saying anything until I see her," I say the truth. "I'm not saying a fucking word about a fucking marriage that is fake to begin with."

"I know that." She points at herself. "And you know that. But they …" She points at the window. "Don't know any of this. To them, you guys were friends who are suddenly married, and they want to be the one who gets the scoop."

"You want to put out a statement," I say, getting up. "We thank you in advance, but this is a private matter and will remain a private matter."

"That is like baiting them," she says. I know she's right, but I can't say anything else right now.

"So then I say nothing," I say. Laurene's phone pings in her hand, and she looks up at me when she sees it.

"What?"

"Just pictures of the two of us," she says, and I shake my head.

"From six years ago when we attended a fucking function?" I ask, going to her, and she holds up her phone.

"More or less." She turns the phone, and it's the one we took last year and then a couple of us on vacation. I read the headline and groan.

A romance undercover. Six signs that they were always together.

"This is why I said you have to say something," Lizzie says. "Or else it's going to be bullshit articles like this, and it can make it worse."

I laugh bitterly. "Make it worse." I shake my head. "How the fuck can it be any worse? The woman who …" I stop myself before I admit to her that I love Becca. I figured that Becca should be the first to hear those words and not someone else. "The woman who I'm actually in a relationship with probably woke up to this shit." I point at the phone. "And I need to get fucking home so I can go and see her."

"I'll pack and be ready." Lizzie looks at me. "We'll get her back," she says, walking out of the room, and the lone tear runs down my cheek.

"Becca," I say her name in a whisper. "Please," I plead with the fucking universe to help me. I get up, packing my shit, and I'm out of the room ten minutes later and so is Lizzie.

"Laurene is going to meet us at home," she says, and I nod at her. I get into the car, looking at my phone to see that no one has texted me back either. The plane is waiting when we arrive. I get out, calling her one last time before I get on the plane. I think at this point I'd be more surprised if she actually answered. I wait for the beep to come.

"Becca." I say her name. "I can explain everything." I walk into the plane, the burn forming in the pit of my stomach. "I'm on my way to you." I press end and look out the window. "I just need one chance to talk to her," I say to myself right before the door of the plane slams shut, and it's almost as if it's her slamming the door on me.

TWENTY-SEVEN

BECCA

THE PLANE TOUCHES down, and I get up. "Looks cold," I tell Erika, grabbing my jacket and putting it over my white cashmere turtleneck. "I might have to run to the mall or something."

"I think there is time," she says, and I look down at my ballerina shoes and so does Erika. "I think we may have to hit up something before we even attempt to go to the rink."

I nod at her, and the phone pings in my hand, one after another. I step out of the plane and make my way over to the car waiting for us. The driver smiles at us and opens the back door. I climb in and take a deep breath before I take out my phone.

I see seventeen missed calls from him and two voice mails. I ignore that, but I can't ignore the text he has just sent me.

Nico: Becca, I need to explain. Let me explain.

I delete it as fast as I can but not fast enough for the pain not to hit me. I grab my sunglasses and place them on, looking out at the cloudy day. It matches how I feel on the inside. If truth be told, all I want to do is curl up and stare into space, but I'm not going to do any of that until tonight. "I got you a suite at the Four Seasons," Erika says from beside me. "It's a regular suite. The top ones were taken."

"That's fine." I look over at her. "My feet are frozen."

"We are stopping at Saks right now," she says, and I nod. We pull up and we both run in, leaving the driver to wait for us. I grab a thicker jacket and also three pairs of UGGs. "I don't think I've ever seen you out of heels." Erika laughs.

We check into the hotel, and then just as quickly as I drop my bag, Erika whisks me out of my room. I think she knows that if I sit, it'll make everything worse. "We have to get to Long Island," she says. I get into the car and see that I have a text from Manning.

Manning: Let me know you're okay.

Me: I'm okay.

Manning: Can I do anything? Do you want to come here?

Me: No, out of town. I'll touch base once I get back home.

Manning: I'm calling you tonight.

I don't answer him. My phone rings, and I see it's Miller. For the first time ever in my career, I send one of my clients to voice mail intentionally. I don't want to do it, but how do I know he isn't with Nico? Instead, I send

Miller a text.

Me: Sorry, in a meeting. Everything okay?

I wait for him to answer, looking out the window as we drive away from the city. "How does the schedule look for tomorrow?"

"We have five kids to see all in and around New York, starting at ten, and I have already ten for Chicago two days from now."

"Good," I say, thinking this is what I need. I need to be buried in my work.

The phone pings, and I see it's Miller.

Miller: Making sure you are okay. Call me when you can.

The car stops, so I put my phone away. I get out of the car and walk into the arena. The smell of ice hits me right away. This is where it starts for all the kids, I think.

I see that the team is already on the ice, and I pull open the doors that have seen better years. The long rink fills the whole room. I walk to the right where I see the metal seats right under the heaters. The smell of teenage boys hit you right away, and it smells like stinky feet and cheddar chips. I stand at the boards watching while Erika is busy on her phone. Her fingers are flying across the keyboard, the sound of the board clattering makes me look on the ice. The boys go at it. "I think you're a little lost." I hear a voice and look up to see Matthew Grant coming close to me. He's dressed in jeans and a leather jacket. I've seen women fall over themselves to get close to him, but his eyes never wander from his wife. From what I've seen and heard, he is madly in love with her.

"Hello there." I smile at him as he comes closer to me. "Fancy seeing you here."

He laughs. "I would say the same since you are far from home." He looks at the ice.

"I was in the neighborhood." He laughs at my joke.

"Seriously." He stands and looks at the players. "You really came all this way to scope out the kids?"

"I wouldn't be the best if I didn't do my homework." I look at the ice. "How's Cooper?"

He puts his hands in his pockets and I see that he is torn. "He's doing good."

"It's hard," I say, and he looks at me. "The whole growing up and them leaving the nest."

"Do you have kids?" he asks, and I shake my head.

"Not yet," I say, and for the first time in my life, I wonder what it would be like if I had kids. The thought knocks me on my ass. "Not anytime soon, either." Erika walks away toward the door as her phone rings. "It also must be hard for him." Matthew just looks at me. "Listen, it's one thing to be good, and everyone wants you." I look toward the ice when I hear the whistle blow. "It's another thing to be fucking good, yet you are constantly compared to everyone in your family."

He nods his head. "Yeah, it sucks for all the kids in the family."

"But from what I've seen," I say. "He is a good kid with a level head on his shoulders."

"He gets that from his mother and less from me." I smile.

"The questions he asked me when we met." I put my

hands into my pockets. "I've never got those questions before. All the kids cared about was the money." He nods his head.

"I have to head out," I say when I see Erika motion with her head. "I have another arena to go to. Say hello to Cooper for me."

"I will," he says, and I walk away from him.

Getting in the car, I don't even bother with my phone. If I am needed, they know to call Erika. By the time we get to the other arena, I'm ready to call it a day.

My ass drags when I get back to my hotel room. Erika is staying in the room right next door to me. I kick off the UGG boots and crawl into the bed fully dressed, looking out the window at the office building in front of it. I don't know how long I lie here, nor do I realize that my pillow is soaking wet from tears when I hear a soft knock on the door. My heart speeds up as I sit up, and I'm about to go the door when it opens.

I walk out of the bedroom, the room dark. I stand here and see Erika is the one coming in, and she turns on the light on the desk. "Oh, hey." She looks at me. "I figured you didn't eat." She pushes the room service cart into the middle of the living room area.

"I'm not really hungry," I say, and she just nods.

"I got you a bowl of soup and a sandwich." She ignores the fact that I just told her I'm not hungry. She takes the silver dome off the food. "I got myself a burger." She shrugs. "Because sometimes you just need to eat a greasy burger."

"Most of the time," I say, walking to the couch. "What

time is it?" I look around to see if there is a clock any-where.

"It's almost nine," she says, and I'm shocked. "Francis and Trevor both called me, all frantic."

I close my eyes, and they suddenly feel so heavy. "I turned off my phone."

"That's what I told them." She grabs her plate. "So take a shower, eat, and then just send them a text."

"Can you?" I ask, and she smiles at me. She turns to walk out of the room.

"Erika." I call her name, and she turns to look at me. "You are going to be a great agent," I say, and her mouth opens in shock. "When we get back, let's try to get your position filled. I don't know if I'm going to find anyone as good."

"Well, we will die trying," she says. "Thank you, Becca, for giving me a chance. I won't let you down." She doesn't say anything else as she walks out. I get up and walk to the bathroom, shrieking at my reflection. My eyes are puffy and red, and my nose is also red. I start the shower, and I look semi alive when I get out. I take two bites of the food, but I'm so tired I walk to bed.

The next day is almost the same. I walk into another arena, this one colder than the last one. I'm sitting down watching when someone sits next to me.

"I'm going to think you are following me," Matthew says, and I smile at him.

"It could be the other way around," I say and look back at the play at hand. "What are you doing here?"

"I wouldn't be a good GM if I didn't check the kids

out myself," he says, and I nod at him. We spend most of the time watching the kids play. "Are you okay?" he asks me.

"What do you mean?" I ask, shocked.

"You look a bit sad," he says. "I noticed it yesterday and well more so today." He turns back and looks at the ice. "I don't mean to pry."

"No." I shake my head. "Just a lot on my mind." I try to sound upbeat. "Plus with the holidays coming up."

He nods his head and gets up. "You're a good one, Becca," he says to me, and all I can do is smirk at him. "My son is going to be in good hands." My mouth hangs open. "I'll be in touch." He turns and walks away. "And if it has anything to do with a man." He smirks. "He's not worth it." I throw my head back and laugh. "It's what I tell my daughters and my nieces."

"Thank you for the advice." I rub my hands on my legs as he walks away.

Erika comes into the arena with two cups of coffee. "Here you go." She hands me one and sits down next to me. "How is it going?"

I look at her, holding the hot cup of coffee in my hand. "Not so good," I say, and I'm not sure if I'm talking about the kids on the ice or myself. "But it'll get better."

She looks at me, not sure what to say. "It will definitely get better."

I get up and walk out of the arena, taking my phone out of my pocket. I have pretty much ignored everyone in the past day and a half, and I'm actually going to give myself another day before I get back on the horse.

I'm getting into the car when the headlines flash on my phone.

Newly married Nico Harrison is spotted coming home without his bride. Is there trouble in paradise already?

TWENTY-EIGHT

Nico

"WHAT THE FUCK is all that?" I say, looking out the window of the plane toward the gate of the airport.

"That," Lizzie says, looking out her own windows, "would be the press." I look back and see maybe fifty people with cameras around their necks. Some of the camera flashes go off.

"What are they doing here?" I get up, grabbing my jacket and putting it on.

"I believe they are here to get a picture," Lizzie says, putting on her own jacket. "I told you before we left that you have to put out a statement." I side-eye at her. "And this is why." She points in the direction of the cameras.

"They have never done this before," I say, grabbing my bag.

"You've never eloped before." She grabs her own bag. "Put on your sunglasses."

I grab my sunglasses and see that Lizzie does the

same. "Here we go," I say as soon as the door opens. I step out the door hear the screaming of the reports.

"Nico, where is your wife? one of them shouts.

"Nico, how long were you together?"

"Nico, is there trouble in paradise?"

"Nico, did you get down on one knee?"

I ignore the questions and try to ignore the camera flashes getting into the waiting car and then taking off my sunglasses. "Well, that wasn't so bad," Lizzie says, huffing as she sits next to me.

"Did you tell the driver I want to go to Becca's place?" I ask, and she turns with her back against the car door.

"Are you insane?" she asks. "You don't think they are going to follow your every single step?"

I look over my shoulder as we drive out of the gate, seeing four or five SUVs following us. "You have two choices." She looks down at her phone and then up at me again. "We can either go home, where there are seven reporters waiting." My mouth hangs open. "Or we can go to the office where there are four reporters."

"I have to go and see Becca," I say. "So drop me off at home and then give me the keys to your car. My patience is running very fucking thin at this point, Lizzie."

"Trust me, I know," she tells me. "But do you want them to get an inkling that you and Becca are linked?" I just look at her. "Do you want them camping out at Becca's house and hounding her and throwing it in her face that you are married and that she's your mistress?"

"She's not the fucking mistress," I hiss out. "She's the actual person I'm with. She's my ..." I don't even know if I should call her my girlfriend.

"Why don't we go home and see if the press gets bored or there is another more entertaining story out there?" She is the voice of reason in this whole thing, and I know that she would not steer me wrong.

"Nico." She says my name softly. "I know that you want to go to Becca." I swallow, and the only thing going through my head is that I'm so close to her, yet I couldn't be more farther from her. "I can only imagine what is going through her mind right now, and my heart hurts for both of you." My fist goes into a ball. "But you have to protect her, and showing up and stomping to her door isn't protecting her."

"Protect her?" I say the words so bitterly. "If this is me protecting her, then what is me hurting her?" My mouth is as dry as the desert in the summer heat.

"I just don't want her to think that what we had ..." Lizzie puts her hand on mine, and she squeezes it.

"Lizzie," I say. "I felt something for her I haven't felt with anyone else," I admit to her. My heart hammers in my chest, the pain becoming stronger and stronger the more I think about how Becca must feel. "She was."

"She is," she corrects me, and I look at her. She has her own tears in her eyes. "Let's see how today goes, and if anything, I will sneak you out tonight."

I don't say anything more. I just swallow the lump in my throat, and when we pull up to the house, the number of reporters seems to have doubled. "Call security and have them off my property," I say to Lizzie, who is already on the phone with them. "I also want people outside the gate."

"I'm ordering it right now," she says, and I walk into the house. I walk up the stairs to the bedroom, and I smell her right away. Walking over to the bed, I sit on her side of the bed. The note I left her two days ago is on the side table. My stomach hurts, the burning starting. Nothing is going to make this go away. The only way this is going to go away is when I see her and hold her in my arms. When I can kiss her and tell her everything.

I hold the note in my hand, hearing Lizzie's steps coming closer and closer. "Okay, so they have been escorted out, and security is parked in front of the house."

"Good," I say, looking at her and then looking down. "How long before I can leave?"

"I would say maybe an hour." I look back down at the note. I take my phone out and send her another message.

Me: I miss you.

The rest of the messages have been of me begging to talk to her. I don't even know if she is reading them or ignoring them. But I'm going to send them to her anyway. Over and over again, just so she knows how much I miss her. How much I need to speak to her. How much I want her. How much I need her.

I look at the screen, hoping the three dots come up, but they don't. Nothing happens. One hour later, I'm sitting in the security guy's car as I drive away from my house. I watch to make sure no one follows me.

I pull up to her building, and my heart hammers in my chest harder than it has ever done before. I take off the baseball hat that I've been wearing and walk into her building. The security man stands. "Hello," I say to him. It's always the same four who man the desk.

"Good evening," he says to me, "who are you visiting?"

"Becca." I smile. "I've been here before."

He grabs the pad that is on the desk. "Can I have a name please?"

"Nico Harrison," I say my name, looking around to make sure no one is watching me from a fucking bush.

"I'm sorry, sir," he says once he looks up. "But you aren't authorized to go up."

"I was here four days ago," I say, and he looks at me.

"If you aren't on the list, I can not let you up," he says, and I just eye him.

"How about you call Becca and see if she will make an exception?" I say, and he nods his head, picking up his phone. He dials her number, my hands in my pockets as I wait for her to answer.

"I'm sorry, there is no answer," he says, putting the phone down. "If you can maybe get her on the phone and have her come down and get you." I nod at him and walk out of her building, knowing she won't answer my calls.

Getting back into the car, I want to punch the steering wheel. I drive back to the house, and Lizzie comes out of the kitchen, her smile disappearing when she sees the look on my face. "I take it that it didn't go well."

"I didn't see her," I say. "She can refuse to see me all she wants. Tomorrow, I'm going to her office."

"Nico." She says my name, and it's more of a warning. "You really want to bring this to her job?"

"She gave me no fucking choice. I have to see her." I turn back and run back to my room, where I can feel her. The whole night, I look up at the ceiling, hugging her pillow in my arms.

I'm up before the alarm, and I'm just shrugging on my gray suit jacket when my phone rings, and I jump at it. I see that it's Miller, and I answer right away.

"Hey," I say, grabbing my keys and walking downstairs. "What's up?"

"Not much. Just getting in the car to head the practice," he says. "You okay?"

"Um," I say, getting in my car and seeing that there are two news vans today waiting for me. "I'm on my way to see Becca."

"Shit," he says. "I've tried to call her, but she just texted me."

"Well, at least she answered you," I say sarcastically. "I'll let you know after I get out of there," I say, disconnecting. I'm so nervous I'm ready to crawl out of my skin.

I drive toward her office and park my car. If anyone is following me, it isn't out of the normal. When I step into the elevator, my palms get sweaty, and if I had eaten anything this morning, I am pretty sure I would have vomited right before I stepped in the elevator. I watch the numbers go from one floor to the next. I bounce on my feet as the elevator doors open, and I walk out. The receptionist smiles at me, and I think this might be a good sign. "Morning," I say. "I'm here to see Becca."

"She isn't here," she says to me. "She's out of town."

My heart fucking sinks to the bottom of the same feet that rushed out of the elevator to see her. "From what I know, I think she is going to be back—"

"Never." I hear from behind me and turn around to see Trevor standing there with Francis beside him.

"You have some fucking brass balls," Francis says, almost hissing at me, and he sees the receptionist just watching as her mouth hangs open.

"We are not doing this here." Trevor is the one who talks. "Follow me," he says, and I wait for them to walk before I follow him to his office. I look at Becca's office that is a bit dark since the lights aren't on. Her assistant's desk is also empty. "Close the door," Trevor says, and I close it, turning to look at them.

"Where is your wife?" Francis hisses at me.

"I'm not doing this with you," I say. "This is between Becca and me."

"There is no you and Becca," Trevor says, and it stings. It fucking hurts.

"The end of you and Becca was the minute you slipped a ring on another woman's finger." I don't tell him that I never slipped anything on anyone. I don't tell them anything because the only person who is going to get my truth is Becca.

"I'm not going anywhere." I stand my ground. "Not now, not tomorrow, not next week. Fuck, not even next month. So when you talk to your sister, you give her that message." I turn to walk out.

"I knew you would come looking for her," Francis says. "I even told her you would." My hand is on the door handle, and I look back, my hand slipping as I turn back and look at him. "She gave me a message for you." I wait, holding my breath. "She said the contract is cancelled."

I glare at him. "Give her a message then. Terms have changed, but the contract is still the same." I turn and walk out of his office, taking out my phone.

Me: Get me my lawyer on the phone now.

TWENTY-NINE

BECCA

"I'M NOT SAYING this out loud," Erika says from beside me. "But I'm fucking happy to go back to wearing shoes and regular jackets."

I laugh. "It has been freakishly cold, hasn't it?" We've been in Chicago for two days and are finally headed to the airport. It's been a rough couple of days and nights. The days pass by slowly, but the nights are the worst. Playing it over and over in my head is what gets me every single time.

The car pulls up to the private plane, and I step out and walk up the four steps as my phone rings in my pocket. I don't rush to it like I used to, but taking the phone out, I see it's Francis.

"Hello." I shrug off my jacket and hand it to the attendant with a smile. "Can I have a water please?" I ask, blocking the phone.

"So he showed up here," he says to me, and my feet

lock in place. "I told you he would, and he did."

"I don't know why," I say in almost a whisper and sit down. I jump when the door slams shut.

"He has a message for you," he says, but I don't want to hear it. I want to tell him I don't want to hear it. My head is screaming at him not to tell me, but my mouth stays shut. "Terms have changed, but the contract is still the same."

"What the fuck?" I whisper out.

"Are you still going to come back?" he asks.

"I'm on the plane, and I'm on my way home. I have nothing to say to him. But I'm done hiding," I say more courageous than I feel. "I'll text you when I land."

I turn off the phone and look out the window. My head is swimming. Why he would show up? What more does he want from me? I grab my phone and type out his name, and I see all the messages he's sent. Every single one is delivered and I want to say unread, but I read them all.

While I lay in bed at night and the memories were too much to bear, I would open the phone and read them. The last one he sent me was this morning.

Nico: *I need to see you.*

My finger rubs over the blue bubble. My head is so lost in thought that I don't even notice when we land. I get up and when I walk out of the plane, the phone beeps again in my hand.

Manning: *Call me please.*

I walk down the steps and dial Manning, who answers right away, his voice going low. "Hey."

"Hey, yourself," I say, walking to the waiting car with the sun hitting me right away. I have to take off the puffy jacket when I get into the car.

"Where are you?" he asks, and I can hear that he's walking.

"Just landed in Dallas," I say. "Is everything okay?"

"Where are you going?" he asks, and I have to wonder if something is wrong.

"I'm on my way home."

"Good. I'll be there in an hour," he says and disconnects. I look back at Erika, who smiles.

"It's good to be home," she says, and I nod, looking out the window.

The doorman opens my door, and I look back over at Erika. "Take the rest of the week off," I say, and she just gasps.

"It's Wednesday," she says, and I laugh.

"I know what day it is." Her face goes into a *yeah right* look. "Okay, fine, I sort of know what day it is."

She laughs. "But we've been going nuts for the last three days. So go to a spa on me and rest up. Monday, we start the search of replacing you as my assistant."

She just smiles so big, and I'm so happy for her. I walk into the building and smile at the security man. "Oh, Ms. Becca, someone was here for you last night," he says, and I stop to look at him. "But his name wasn't on the list."

"Did he say who he was?" I ask, knowing that it was Nico. Who else could it have been?

"A Mr. Harrison" he says, and I swallow the lump. "I

tried to call you, but …"

"That's okay," I say to him. "Actually, from now on, I'd like all guests announced."

"Of course," he says to me, and I walk to the elevator. I press the button and finally walk into my house.

Making my way upstairs, I get out of the warm clothes and slip on a pair of yoga pants and a top. I'm making myself a coffee when the phone rings. "Hello?" I say.

"There is a Manning who is here to see you," the security guard says.

"Send him up," I say and hang up the phone. I walk over to the door and open it right when he steps off the elevator. He looks over at me, and his smile turns into a frown.

"When is the last time you ate?" He comes to me and gives me a hug. I try to be strong, but the lump forms in my throat. He lets me go, and I wipe the tear coming out of the corner of my eye with my thumb. He takes out his phone and then looks at me. "I just ordered us lunch."

"You didn't have to do that," I say, and we walk into the house.

"I know that, but I wanted to," he says softly. I sit on the couch, and he sits on the couch in front of me.

"This has to be the most awkward I've ever felt around you," I say, and he laughs.

"More awkward than seeing naked photos of my wife having sex with someone else?" he jokes, and I laugh.

"Okay, fine, that was a little bit more awkward," I admit to him.

"How are you?" He leans forward, putting his elbows

on his knees.

"I'm good," I lie, and he knows it. "Okay, fine. I'm not good, okay?" I wring my hands together. "I'm mad. I'm angry. I'm pissed off, and I'm fucking sad."

He shakes his head. "I have no idea what he was thinking."

I put my hands up. "I don't even want to put you in that position. You are not going to be put in the middle of this."

"I'm not," he says. "He fucked up," he admits. "I might have told him that to his face."

"Manning." I say his name.

"No, Becca," he sighs. "It's fucked up. We saw you two days before. He was the one who laid down his claim, and then he goes and marries someone else. What in the ever-loving fuck is going on?"

My bottom lip trembles. "He …" I say, "he was obviously not in it as much as I thought."

"I saw him," Manning cuts me off. "I saw how he looked at you. You can't fake that."

"Well then, I guess he's a really good actor," I say, sitting more into the couch and curling my feet under me. "Honestly, we were together the night before," I admit to him. "I knew something was off. He was acting weird, but I thought it was just work."

"So when did you find out?" he asks.

"The morning when the headlines came out while I was on the treadmill," I admit to him, and he gets up.

"I'm going to fucking kill him!" he shouts, grabbing his phone out of his pocket.

I jump off the couch, not ready for Nico to know I'm home. I am not delusional in thinking we can avoid each other, but it gives my heart more time to forget him. "Stop," I say, and his hand stops. "Please, he doesn't know I'm home and …"

He tosses his phone on the couch. "Oh, he and I are going to have fucking words. I can tell you that."

"Well, good news is he can't fire you." I try to joke with him, and he doesn't crack a smile.

"I don't know how you are doing it," he says, and I sit back down.

"Full transparency," I say. "It's been rough. The nights are worse than the days." I swallow. "I was in love with him." His mouth opens, but he doesn't have time to say anything before there is a knock on the door, and I fly up, afraid it's Nico.

"I got it," he says. "Stay here." I nod at him and watch him walk out of the room. He comes back two seconds later with a brown bag. The smell makes my mouth water. "It's just food."

He sets the bag on the middle of the coffee table, taking the fries out and then handing me a burger. "Thank you," I say, sitting on the floor in front of the coffee table. "For doing this." He sits down in front of me. "For checking on me."

"Becca," he says my name and I look at him. "You are one of my closest friends. What you did for me, there is nothing I can do to pay you back."

"Well, consider us even," I say, unwrapping the burger and wiping the tear that runs down my cheek with the back of my hand. I take a bite of the burger and we don't talk for the rest of the meal. Neither of us says anything.

"Will you call me if you need anything?" Manning asks after we've cleaned up the food, and I'm walking him to the door.

"I will," I say, and he just looks at me. "Okay, fine, I really will." I laugh. "If at any time, I need something or anything, I will call you."

"I know you're lying," he says and takes me in his arms to give me a hug. "But I'm going to pretend you aren't."

I watch him walk out of the apartment and close the door after he steps into the elevator. I close the door, and the sound of my phone fills the room. I walk over to it and pick it up, seeing Nico's name.

I look at it for longer than I should. My finger hovers over the green button, but I press the decline button. "Not today," I tell the phone, my stomach lurching.

My phone bings with a text, and I see it's from him. It doesn't stop with just one either. It is one after another.

Nico: I just need to see you for five minutes.

Nico: Becca. Please.

Nico: I just need to see that you are okay.

I turn the phone off. After powering it down, I get up and walk to the bathroom. I turn on the water for the bath, turning back around and going to get my phone. Turning it back on, I pretend I'm doing it for work. I pretend I'm doing it because it's the only lifeline I have to him. I pretend until the tears come. I pretend until I finally sob out with the need of wanting him.

THIRTY

Nico

"**W**HERE THE FUCK is my lawyer?" I look over at Lizzie, who looks up from her phone. "It's been two fucking days."

"He was on vacation. He'll be here in thirty minutes. I asked him to come after everyone left, just in case someone is listening," she says, setting her phone down. I get up to look out my office window. The sun is slowly setting, it's the part of the day I start to hate. The days are bearable, just barely, but the nights. The nighttime is my enemy. The memories are the worst. It's almost like my penance for everything I've done. I walk around my room, trying to forget, except the memories come back full force. The minutes feel like hours. The hours feel like days. The days feel like years.

"I pay him enough to be here when I need him," I say, putting my hands in my pockets. "When are we leaving?"

"Tomorrow afternoon," she says. "But we get back tomorrow night." My eyes focus on the car lights starting to fill up the streets. The Christmas streetlights are starting to light up. "Then there are four more days, and then you are gone for the whole week right before we break for Christmas." I close my eyes at the mention of Christmas, making my heart pound. "I'm assuming you aren't going to any of the parties we got invitations for." I just look over my shoulder, and she holds up her hands. "Don't shoot the messenger. Is she back?" she asks quietly, and I nod.

"She got back home yesterday," I say. "Manning told me." I don't tell her that he came to see me, and it wasn't pleasant. I also don't tell her that when he left, I punched a hole in my wall. I don't tell her that when he left, I called Becca twenty-five times, and she never answered once. I don't tell her that I took a bottle of scotch to bed with me.

"Has she …?" I shake my head, the lump forming in my throat. I'm almost tempted to camp out in her lobby and wait for her.

"Not even a text," I say and then I hear heels clicking and turn to look at the door. I know it isn't her, but my heart somehow hopes it is. Even if she yells at me and kicks me in the balls, I will give anything to see her again. Even if it's just for two minutes. Just enough time to tell her everything that I feel.

"Well, well, well," Laurene says, walking into the office. She is dressed in a pantsuit with heels. She smiles at Lizzie and goes to sit next to her. "Is someone going to tell me why I've been summoned here?"

I don't get a chance to tell her because there is a knock on the door, and I turn to see my lawyer standing there. I look at him with a scowl. "About fucking time you showed up, George."

"Nico," Lizzie warns with a low voice.

"I was on vacation," he says, coming in. "I told you this as soon as I married you."

"Yeah, well, shit happens," I say, and he just stares at me. The both of us were in college at the same time. We were in the same circle, and when he became a lawyer, I was his first client. Of course he joined his father's firm that was started five generations before. He's one of the biggest names out there. "I pay you enough to be at my beck and call."

"And I was available," he says, going to the empty chair and sitting down in it. The girls smile at him. "Now what was so pressing?"

"I need you to go through Laurene's contract," I say, and Laurene's eyes go big.

"Um, hold on a minute." She puts up her hand. "My lawyer went through it with a fine-tooth comb."

"I need you to find a loophole for this marriage," I tell George. "There has to be something in there."

"Oh my God," Laurene says, throwing her hand up and having it slap the arm of the couch. "Seriously, it's for ninety fucking days, Nico."

"Yeah, and it's ninety days too long," I say, and she shakes her head.

"What is the sudden freaking rush to get divorced?"

she asks, and then I look at her and then at Lizzie, who just shrugs, not sure what to say. "You knew this."

"I did, and you know that I only married you because of a fucking promise I made when we were both eighteen and drunk," I point out.

"Where is the contract?" George asks. Lizzie grabs her leather binder case and takes it out, handing it to him. He reaches over and grabs it. "I'm going to go over this and then bring it to a couple of people to make sure I don't miss anything."

"Is that the same people from your firm who leaked that we were married?" George glares at me.

"Don't insult the people standing in your corner," he says, getting up. "I'll be in touch." He walks out of the room, closing the door behind him.

"Nico," Laurene says. "I honestly don't know what has gotten into you."

"This marriage has ruined my life," I say. "Literally and figuratively ruined my fucking life."

"I don't understand." She looks at me, getting up.

"I was dating someone when you came to me," I finally tell her, and Lizzie gets up and comes over to me. She grabs my hand and squeezes it.

"Okay," Laurene says, not sure she is understanding what I'm saying. The truth be told, I don't even know what I want to say. All the words just spin around and around in my head.

"I'm in love with her," I say, and her mouth opens, then closes, and then opens again. "Like in love with her so much I would trade everything I have to see her for one more minute."

"Did you tell her?" she asks in a whisper and then sits back on the couch again.

"No." I run my hands through my hair. "I didn't know how much to tell her. Then I didn't know how to tell her." Laurene puts her hand to her chest. "I was going to tell her when I got back."

"Are you telling me, Nico, that the woman you love." She gets up, and I can see she is angry. "Or that you say you love." Putting her hands on her hips, she continues, "Found out you married me after the fact that you married me?"

"Oh, it's better than that," Lizzie says, side-eyeing me with a glare. "She found out when the press broke the story."

"How can you be so fucking smart?" She shakes her head. "Yet so fucking dumb?"

"I don't need this right now," I tell them both.

"No, you don't," Lizzie says. "But it's about time someone said it out loud."

"I didn't want any of this." Throwing my hand up in the air, I say, "None of it. And truth be told, I knew I liked her. Like a lot, but the fact that I love her. It shocked me."

"You fucked up," Laurene tells me. "And not just a little bit."

"I know you don't think I know I fucked up," I tell them both. "You think I don't want to turn back time and just come out and tell her."

"I don't even know what to say or what to ask," Laurene says, sitting down. "When was the last time you saw her?"

"The day before we got married," I tell them, and I can see Laurene glare. "I know what you are going to say, and trust me, I've had this talk with myself over and over again. Night after fucking night. I just couldn't tell her. Besides, I didn't want to break your trust."

"My trust," Laurene says softly. "You have to know that I would have trusted you to tell her. I assume that you aren't involved with someone who runs to the press."

"Of course not," I say, defending her. "Fuck, she didn't even want to tell anyone we were involved. I was the one who kissed her in front of people."

"This," Lizzie says and then looks over at Laurene, who finishes the sentence for her.

"It gets worse and worse," she says. "Where is she now? Did she give you an ultimatum? Is that why you are going crazy to get this divorce?"

I shake my head. "She hasn't said a word to me. Every single voice mail is unanswered. Every single text sits on the screen."

"Well, she has class, that is for sure," Laurene says, and I look at her. "What?" she questions me.

"You don't even know her," I point out.

"I don't have to know her," she says. "I know that she woke up one morning and found out you were married and didn't come to your house and bust every single window. She hasn't come here demanding that you answer her. She hasn't gone to the press and sold her story." She stops talking, and I just look at her. "And let's be honest, that story would sell for millions."

"She isn't like that," I say. "She would never bring anything negative to her. She is kind and loyal. The last thing she would do is make a scene or make the press aware of it. No, not my girl," I say, the pressure on my chest hitting me when I say my girl. "She is not going to do that. She would never do that."

"You need to get her to listen to you," Lizzie says, and I just stare at her.

"Wow, I didn't think of that," I tell them both sarcastically. "I wish it was that easy."

"I'm in shock," Laurene says. "Complete and utter shock. One, that you were with someone. Two, that you love this person, and three, that you are a dumbass."

"This isn't helping anyone," I point out to her. "I just hope that there is a loophole."

"And then what?" she asks, folding her hands over her chest.

"And then we get annulled," I say.

"Oh my God," Lizzie says. "You think that is going to solve this problem."

"He's such a man," Laurene says, getting up and grabbing her purse. "Us being married is the least of your problems. Even if we annul the marriage, you think she is going to talk to you?"

"I have to try," I say softly. "I have to try whatever I can to get her to see me. I don't want to think of being without her. I don't want to think about not being able to hold her or touch her or laugh with her. It's unimaginable, and every single time I think about it, I get this pressure in the middle of my chest, and it won't go away," I finally admit out loud. "I can't sleep. I can't eat. I can't live without her."

They don't say anything to me because there is nothing to say. Nothing will make me feel better. Nothing they could do will make the pain go away. There is nothing anyone can do. Only one person can make this all better. Only one person can put me out of my misery.

Becca.

She is the only one in all of this who can make me whole again, yet the only person who will not give me the time of day.

THIRTY-ONE

BECCA

"WELCOME BACK," TREVOR says to me when I walk into my office. I look over my shoulder at him.

"I said I was coming in on Monday." I set down my coffee on the desk and slip off my brown cashmere coat. "And it's Monday."

He nods. "How are you feeling?" he asks, and I shrug.

"I've been better," I say, and it's the truth. What I don't tell him is that instead of getting easier, it gets fucking harder. Every single day, he calls morning, noon, and night. I'm thinking he will eventually get tired of calling. I keep hoping that he doesn't send me anymore texts, yet I look for them. I scroll through them in the middle of the night when I wake yearning for him.

"Well, you look like you need to eat," he says, and I roll my eyes.

I'm not going to say the black leather skirt I'm wearing is loose on me. It's the reason I paired it with the green V-neck short-sleeved top that is loose and ties around the waist. It hides everything. "I eat," I say. "Is Francis in?"

"He's going to be here at nine," Trevor says.

"Okay, why don't we meet in the conference room to go over a couple of things? Mainly New York and Chicago."

"Sounds good," he says. I sit down and open my computer, seeing that Erika took care of everything that needs to be taken care of. She walks into my office thirty minutes later. "Your brothers are ready," she says, smiling at me. I get up, grabbing my coffee. "Thank you for taking care of everything last week. Even though I gave you the rest of the week off," I tell her, and she just nods her head.

"You know me," she says, and I don't have to answer her. I know exactly the type of person she is. I was that person.

I fill my brothers in on who I want to go after, and they all agree with me. The day passes with me making sure I have everything ready to go when the time is right. Lunch comes and goes. Erika has a sandwich delivered, and when she sticks her head back into my office, I notice that it is getting dark outside. "I'm about to head out," she says, and I nod. "Don't stay too late."

"I won't," I say, looking down. I start to get up when I hear heels clicking toward my office, and I smile, shaking my head. "What did you forget?" I walk out of my office and come face-to-face with Laurene. The only reason I know who this person is because of the front news pictures that went on. She stands there in a pantsuit with stunning shoes. Her blond hair is tied up in the back of her head in a bun. Her makeup is perfect, and it's hard to admit that she really is beautiful.

"I'm sorry to interrupt, but I was looking for Becca," she says, smiling at me. My hands start to shake just a touch. I never thought I would come face-to-face with the woman who is married to the man I love. Fuck, no one would even believe me.

"You've found her," I say, my voice coming out without a tremble, and I even impress myself.

"I'm Laurene," she says, putting out her hand for me to shake it, and my hand automatically extends. "I was hoping I could have a couple of minutes of your time."

I look around the office, making sure who is here. I am not one to get physical, but if she touches even a hair on my head, I'm going to drop her. Period. I move away from the door so she can walk in. "Please." I motion with my hand.

She walks in, and I close the door behind her. "This I …" I say. "Um."

"It's not every day that you meet the wife of the man who you love." She laughs and I just look at her. "I was trying to break the ice. I try to be funny when I'm nervous."

"Please have a seat." I point at the couch and walk over to one of the chairs that faces the couch. My hands and knees both trembling. "What can I do for you?"

"I was hoping we could talk, woman to woman," she says, and she puts her hands on her knees. "I don't suppose you know who I am."

I take a deep breath. "I'm sorry I haven't read your biography, if that is what you're asking."

She tilts her head. "I like you. Lizzie said I would."

"I'm sorry." I start to get up. "But I really have nothing to say to you right now."

"That's quite all right. That means I can do all the talking." I stand straight.

"I'm not sure I want to hear what you have to say," I answer her honestly.

"I met Nico when we were both seven." My stomach starts to sink, and I don't know how much I can't stand. "We were both dressed in our Sunday best even though it was Friday. There was some event that we couldn't miss, and we had no choice but to be there. That was us for basically our whole life. At every single function, the two of us would be left in the corner to fend for ourselves while everyone danced and was seen." She swallows. "My father is CEO for Night & Day Industries. It was handed down to him from his father and so on. It goes back five generations. I thought it was my legacy, I thought it was going to be passed down to me. I waited. Counted the days. I worked my ass off to take it over, and when it was time for my father to retire, he names my cousin as his predecessor. He had no idea what the company stood for. He had no idea about how the company ran, what he did know was how to snort coke off his mistress's ass." I stand here shocked. "And other places. He was the perfect child, prim and proper in front of the eyes, but an asshole behind closed doors."

"I don't know what to say," I say honestly. "I also don't know what this has to do with me."

"Well, when I was looked over, I was a wreck, a mess. I'm talking snot crying with vengeance I would make them pay. So Nico, being the friend that he was, sat with me while I downed one shot of tequila after another. I vowed I would make them pay. I would show them what a mistake they made." She looks down and then looks back up again and she has tears running down her face. "My father died two weeks later. Although he didn't leave me his company, he left me his stock options. For the past ten years, I've been slowly working my way up to buying a majority of the stocks to take over the company that is rightfully mine. With that said, there was one family who I needed, and no matter how many fucking times I wined and dined them, the one thing stopping them from selling it to me. I was an unmarried woman."

I want to roll my eyes. "Harold, the father, was adamant that I have a man by my side to guide me. He was also holding out because he would have liked me to be married. Can you believe we are in the twentieth-first century and a woman cannot be without a man?"

"I'm sorry that you went through all that," I say. "Truly I am, but—"

"I tried everything to get him to sell them to me, and when I say everything, I mean everything. He wouldn't budge so I called in Nico. I begged him to help me out. He was hesitant at first and even he tried to get him to switch without actually having to get married but." My mind starts to spin when she starts to talk about Nico's part in this plan. "It was supposed to be a ninety-day marriage. We had the lawyer draft up NDAs for anyone who was on the case to sign. It was never, ever supposed to be leaked." The tear that is waiting to fall finally rolls over. "For that, I'm so, so sorry."

"I'm …" I say, and my throat closes up.

"I don't know what you and Nico had," she says. "But I do know that my best friend is suffering. I have never seen him like this, and to be honest, I had no idea about you until yesterday when he almost tore off his lawyer's head," she says.

"Then he confessed to me what happened and I have to be honest. He's a smart man, but he's also a very stupid man." I almost laugh at her. "But he's also kind and so fucking loyal he married me just so I can get stocks in a company." I try to say something. I try to, but nothing comes out. My mouth is dry, and as much as I try not to cry in front of her, I can't stop the one tear that escapes.

"I know what it feels like to love someone and they not know." She wipes her own tear. "I fell in love with Lizzie when I was thirteen. I didn't know then that it would be a love that would seep so deep in me that nothing would come close to it." My eyes go wide, my mouth hangs down. "I kissed her for the first time three years ago. No one knows that we are together, not even Nico. I love her with everything I have, and I have no idea how I would be if I had to stand back and watch her parade around with someone. I can't imagine what you went through when you found out. I would never want to inflict that pain on anyone." She wipes her tear away.

"It's not your fault," I say, and she gets up.

"I won't take up anymore of your time," she says, turning and walking away. She stops when she gets to the door. "Nico also doesn't know that I'm here right now."

"Why?" I ask. "Why come here and plead his case?"

"Because regardless of what happens, you should know that we aren't together like that," she says. "The marriage is as fake as my boobs." I want to burst out laughing, but I can't. "I hope to see you soon."

She turns and walks out of my office. I stand here for a second until my legs give out, and I fall into the chair.

I don't even focus when I make my way home. I walk to my room and undress, slipping into jeans. I'm walking downstairs when I make the decision to end this. End all of this. I get into the car, my head replaying Laurene's words. Over and over again, I fight back the tears.

Getting out of the car, I look around, seeing only a couple of lights on. I walk up to the door and press the doorbell. I wrap my jacket closer to me as my heartbeat echoes in my ears. I hear footsteps and then the lock unlocking. I have been practicing this moment. I've seen it in my head, but nothing could have prepared me for this.

The door is pulled open and all I can do is look at him. "Becca," he whispers. He stands there in his dress pants and a white shirt that I know is almost soft like silk. His two buttons at his neck are open, his sleeves rolled up. His hair looks like his hands were just in them, his eyes look exactly like mine. With heavy circles around them and the light in them gone.

"Nico," I say, feeling almost like a stranger standing in front of him. "I was wondering if you had a minute to talk."

THIRTY-TWO

Nico

"Nico." SHE SAYS my name, and my heart stops in my chest. She's so fucking beautiful she takes my breath away. "I was wondering if you had a minute to talk."

"Come in," I say. I want to pull her into the house. I want to pull her into my arms. I want to pull her to me, grab her face, and kiss her lips. The whole day has been shot to shit. We left yesterday for the game, and for the first time ever, I had no emotion for it. I was there, but my head was back here in Dallas, wondering how she was.

She walks in, and I take her in. My memory is nothing compared to the real thing. "I don't want to interrupt you," she says, and I can see that she's nervous, and I hate it. I hate all of this fucking shit.

"You can never interrupt me," I say to her and I hope she looks up at me again. But she just looks down, and I'm internally roaring in madness. "Can I get you something to drink?" I ask, hoping it will keep her here longer if only for one minute more.

"I think I'm okay." She laughs, but you know it's a fake laugh. Her eyes don't light up, and her smile doesn't fill her face. "I don't want to take anymore of your time."

"Becca," I say her name in almost a plea. The minute I say her name, I see the tears fill her eyes, and if I thought I knew pain before, I was wrong. The sight of her in this state is more than I can cope with. The fact that I made her feel like this. I feel like someone has cracked open my chest and pulled out my heart. "Let's go into the living room."

She blinks away the tears and follows me. The last time I was in this room with her, she was naked and in my arms. I wait for her to sit before taking a seat. "I've been calling you," I say, and she nods her head. "I'm so sorry, Becca." The lump forms even bigger in my throat when I see her trembling hand wipe away a tear.

"Well …" She shakes her head and looks down at her trembling hands. I want to get up to go over to her and hold her hands in mine. "Laurene came to see me." She shocks me with those words.

"When she came to me, I thought she was joking, to be honest," I say. Whatever happens, she has to hear the truth, and she has to hear it from me. "But then I went with her to a meeting, and I knew the guy wasn't going to budge." I knew that if anything would come out of this, you would at least hear it from me.

"I just …" Her voice trembles. "I just don't understand why you didn't tell me."

I shake my head, the pit of burning starting in my stomach. "I wanted to. The night that you came over for dinner."

"I knew something was bothering you," she points out to me. "I asked you, and you said it was nothing."

"I was a coward," I admit. "I didn't know how to bring it up."

"You think me finding out when I turned on the television is better than hearing it from you," she says bitterly.

"I wanted to tell you in person," I say, and she shakes her head. "It's just how do you bring up the fact that you have to marry someone for ninety days while you're with your new girlfriend?" I get up, the nerves running through me. "It's not exactly 'hey, can you pass the salt, oh, and by the way, I'm getting married tomorrow.'"

"Well." She stands, and I see she's angry. "It's fucking better than turning on the television and finding out that way, I can tell you that much."

"I'm so sorry," I say, my voice coming out in almost a whisper.

"How would you feel," she starts, "if you woke up one day, and the news is all over that I was married to Manning?"

"I would kill," I answer honestly, the blood in my veins running cold.

"I keep thinking about it over and over in my head," she says. "Everything that Laurene told me, and I am going to be one-hundred percent honest with you right now. If the roles were reversed, I would have done the same."

"What?" I ask, shocked.

"If I had to marry one of my clients for whatever reason, I would do it. If it hurt no one," she adds at the end. "That is what gets me the most. I would have understood. I might not have liked it, but you didn't even give me a chance." She points at herself.

"I wish I could go back," I say softly. "I wish I could go back to the beginning and tell you from the start. I have never regretted anything more in my life," I say, and she nods her head. "What I feel for you, it's something."

"I love you," she cuts me off, and my heart feels like it's going to jump out of my chest. "I just didn't know it until it was too late."

"It's not too late," I say, the dread creeping into me. I walk over to her, and she doesn't move away. I put my hand on her face. "It's not too late." My thumb rubs the tear away from her cheek that escaped. "Please, Becca. I love you."

"Which makes this suck even more than I thought it would," she says.

"We can make it work." I will get down on my knees and beg her to stay with me. "I will do whatever." I put my forehead on hers.

"But the thing is," she says, "I can't get over the fact you didn't tell me." She puts her hands on mine and slowly steps out of my reach. "In this whole thing, you never put me before anything."

"You're the only thing I thought about," I say. "The only thing that ran through my mind."

"Yet you couldn't tell me," she says. "You couldn't

just be honest with me. That is something I can't get over. I can't be just an afterthought." She looks down. "I'm sorry. I just can't forgive that. For my whole life, I was pushed to the side and not thought of. I can't be with someone who treats me the same way."

"There is nothing that I can say that will change your mind?" I don't know if I'm asking her or telling her.

She shakes her head. "I wanted you to know that I get the whole marriage thing. But I don't get the secret thing, especially from me. We were in a relationship. I was supposed to be your partner."

"I'm so sorry." It's the only thing I can think to say.

"Me, too," she says, taking a deep breath. "More than you know." We stare at each other. "I'll see myself out," she says, walking past me. I call her name one last time.

"Becca." I say her name, and she looks over her shoulder. "You are worth everything." She smiles sadly at me, not hiding the tear running down her face this time.

"So are you, Nico," she says right before she walks out of the room. I listen to her footsteps, getting farther and farther away from me. The pain in my chest gets stronger and stronger until I can't stand it anymore, and I drop to my knees at the same time as the door slams shut.

I hear her car door, and I get up in time to look out the window and see the red lights fade into the distance. Turning, I go over to the bar and grab the bottle of scotch. I don't bother with a glass.

I drink until the burning down my throat stops. I sit here until I hear more footsteps, and this time, I see Lizzie and Laurene walk into the room. "Oh, this is fun,"

Lizzie says, coming over and sitting down in front of me.

"Was that bottle full?" Laurene asks, walking in and sitting next to Lizzie.

"You went to see Becca," I say. "She came here."

"I did," Laurene says and then looks over at me. "I wanted her to know that you had no choice."

I don't say anything else. I just take another drink. "Getting drunk is not going to help you get her back," Lizzie says to me.

"That ship has sailed," I tell them. "It's over." The words taste so bitter in my mouth. "She can't be with someone who doesn't think about her."

"I'm so sorry," Laurene says, getting up and walking over to me. "I thought if she knew the whole story."

"Oh, she gets the whole story." I laugh bitterly. "She said she would have done the same. What she can't forgive is my not even thinking about how she would feel."

"I'm sure once she has time to sort through it all," Lizzie says, trying to make me feel better, but I just look over at her.

"It's done." The words get stuck in my throat.

"I'm so sorry," Laurene says. "This is all my fault."

"Um, no, it's not," Lizzie says, going to her and putting her arm around her shoulder. "He should have told her what was going on."

Laurene puts her hand on Lizzie's leg, and she smiles up at her. "What the fuck is going on right now?" I point at both of them.

They look at each other again and then look at me. "Well, we have some news," Lizzie says, beaming.

"We're getting married!" I gasp.

"Maybe we should have started with we are together before telling him we are getting married," Laurene says, kissing her.

"What?" I sit up. "When?" I don't wait for them to answer "How?" I look back and forth at them. "Where?"

"I've been in love with her for seven years," Laurene says, looking at Lizzie.

"I've been telling myself that I'm not good enough for her for seven years," Lizzie says to her. "Luckily, we got drunk one night, and the next thing you know, she's riding—" I put my hand up.

"I don't want to know." I get up and look at them. "I'm happy for you."

I walk out of the room, the smell of Becca still lingering in the air. My heart falling when I walk into my bedroom and I see that the cleaning lady washed the sheets. Walking over to the bed, I stand here looking at the spot where she used to sleep. "Becca," I whisper her name, falling on the bed. I bring the pillow to my nose and moan when it doesn't smell like her anymore. "Becca," I call her name, praying that somehow she can hear me. "Becca," Again and again, I say her name until the darkness takes me.

THIRTY-THREE

BECCA

I ROLL OUT of bed, my whole body hurting from the top of my head right down to my toes. I skipped another morning run, and at this point, I don't even care. It's been over a week since I last saw Nico. The calls stopped after that night as did the texts.

I don't know what I was expecting. I told him it was over, so why would he still send me messages and texts. I walk over to the coffee machine, pressing the button, then I turn on the television. The sports news makes me look up, and I lie to myself, thinking that I'm doing it for my clients.

Instead, I wait to see any shots of Nico. I turn off the television after the guy stops talking about the Oilers because I'm not interested in the other games. I walk up to my bedroom, and I get dressed. I grab my beige knit checkered skirt that wraps around so I can make it fit on my body. The weight I lost has not come back. I grab my long-sleeved cashmere sweater with gold buttons down the front, then slip on the caramel suede booties.

I just stare at myself in the mirror. "When is the last time you were happy?" I ask myself, and I know the answer. "When was the last time you smiled?" Is the next question. "When was the last time you did something for you?"

I walk away from the mirror, grabbing a Starbucks before work. I walk into the office, and it's like a switch flips in me. "Erika," I say once I get closer to my office. "Can you tell my brothers I need to have an emergency meeting?"

"Sure," she says, and she picks up the phone. I walk into my office and take my wraparound shawl off and sit at my desk. Turning my chair, I look out the window. "They said they can do it now."

"Perfect," I say, smiling and getting up. "I'd like you to attend also."

She nods at me, and we walk to the conference room. Trevor is right behind me, followed by Francis.

"I'm almost afraid of this meeting," Francis says, sitting down in one of the empty seats, and I laugh.

I look at them and smile. "Guys." I swallow.

"She's pregnant," Trevor says. "Fuck."

"How can she be pregnant and lose fifty pounds?" Francis says.

"Okay, one, I'm not pregnant," I say. "Two, I lost fifteen pounds, not fifty. But I am leaving."

"Leaving?" they both say at the same time. I look over at Erika, who looks at me in shock.

"More of a sabbatical than anything else." I smile for the first time in a long time. "Erika is going to take over for me since she knows all of my clients."

"Where are you going to go?" Trevor asks.

"I have no idea," I tell them honestly. "Somewhere warm where I can sit on the beach."

"But this isn't forever," Francis says. I shake my head and the tear comes out.

"It's not forever. It's …" I look around the table. "I'm not happy," I admit. "And I don't like myself not happy. I miss the old me who used to be happy to get up and run on the treadmill. I miss the old me that used to come into work and dive right in. I miss the old me who didn't have a broken heart." I haven't told my brothers the secret about Nico and his fake wedding. I haven't told anyone because it's not my story to tell, and I would never betray him like that. "I just need a new start."

"Whatever you need," Erika says.

"Thank you," I say. "Now, I'm not just going to up and leave. I'll finish this week. I will tell my closest clients, but other than that, if you need anything, I will always be just a phone call away."

"What do we tell people?" Trevor asks.

"I'll send out an email to everyone, letting them know I'm going on a sabbatical, and we can go from there." I look around the table. "Let's send it out on Friday at five o'clock, so people have the weekend to ask us questions."

"If this is what you want," Francis says. "We're not going to stop you."

"Who knows." I put up my hands. "Maybe I'll be bored out of my mind and rush back after a week."

Trevor gets up and comes over to hug me. "Take all the time you need," he says, kissing my cheek, and Francis follows next. They walk out, and I look over at Erika, who has her own tears.

"Are you crazy?" She looks at me. "I can't do your job."

"Oh, yes, you can," I say to her. "Probably better than me, and who knows, maybe no one will miss me," I say as we walk out of the conference room.

I pick up my phone and call Manning. "Hey." He answers right away.

"Hi, there." I try to sound chipper. "I was wondering if you were free today or tomorrow? I don't need a lot of time. It could even be done over coffee."

"Yeah, how about I swing by the office? I'm on my way to the rink," he says. "See you in ten."

I hang up the phone and wait for him. When he comes walking in ten minutes later, I get up and go to him. "Thank you so much," I say and close the door behind him. He looks at me and takes off his baseball cap. "For coming so fast."

"Going to be honest, I am a little scared, especially with the door being closed." He laughs nervously as he sits down on the couch.

"Everything is fine," I say, sitting down. "I mean, it's going to be fine."

"Are you dying?" he asks, the worry all over his face, and I laugh loud.

"I'm not dying," I say, "but I am leaving." He just looks at me. "I'm taking a sabbatical, and I don't know for how long."

"Fuck," Manning says. "I told Nico I would fuck him up." I shake my head.

"Please don't do that," I say. "It's really a me thing."

"What can I do?" he asks sincerely. "How can I help?"

"Right now, I'm coming to terms with being in love and not being able to do anything about it," I say honestly, "and I'm tired of being sad and mad. I think I need to get away."

"You need to eat, pray, love," he says, shaking his head, and for the first time in a long time, I laugh so much my stomach hurts.

I hug him goodbye and walk back to my desk. Picking up my phone, I call Francis. "What is the nicest beach you've been to?"

"Thailand," he says. "You aren't going to Thailand alone, so Turks and Caicos."

"I can go to Thailand by myself," I say, "but I'm not going to because I like Turks." I hang up the phone with him, and in a matter of an hour, I have a villa booked in Turks. That night, I pack my stuff.

"Hey," Erika says, poking her head into my office. "Are you ready to go over the email?" she asks. She has hit the ground running. I've told Manning, Miller, and Ralph as well as some others.

"I have it all written," I say. "I am just waiting for five o'clock to press send."

"What time does your plane leave?" Erika asks.

"Six." I smile at her. "My bags are already packed and waiting for me at home."

"I can't believe you're doing it," she says, sitting down in one of my chairs. She is moving into her own office on Monday, and even though she didn't want to, I put my foot down and forced her to.

"I'm doing it," I say. My heart is a little sad I'm leaving right before the holidays, but I'm happy to be out of here. "This time tomorrow, I'll be sinking into a hammock and listening to the water." I wink at her. "And who knows, I could meet someone who is mending a broken heart, and we can fall madly in love." I know I'm exaggerating, but it was fun to say.

"Okay, I'm really jealous," she says.

"Do you want me to read the email?" I ask, and she nods her head, tears forming in her eyes again. "You act like I'm dying, and you will never see me again."

"It's just," she says, "since the first day I've started here, you've been my hero and someone who I look up to every single day."

"Aw," I say, touched by her words. "You cannot make me cry." I raise my hand. "I do enough of that shit on my own," I joke with her. I have to admit, it's becoming less and less frequent, and I thought that was a good thing, but the pain in my chest lingers, and some days, the pain feels like an actual stab wound.

"Okay, fine, before we are both blubbering messes, how about you read me the email."

I smile at her, opening the document and reading it to her. By the end of the short letter, I have my own tears.

I look at my watch. "It's almost time." I get up and hug her. "I'm going to head out before it goes out," I say. "Can you send it?"

"Of course," she says, and I smile. "I'm going to miss you."

"I'll send pictures," I say, and she walks out of the office. Trevor and Francis already came to say goodbye. I take one look around the office before grabbing my purse. Stopping by the doorway, I turn the lights out, and my heart sinks just a touch.

I smile at everyone. No one knows what is going to come at five o'clock, but it was what I wanted. I didn't want the whole goodbye hugs and all that. I am coming back. I had to argue with Trevor and Francis, so it's silly. "Have a nice weekend!" someone yells to me, and I turn to smile at them.

"You as well." I walk out before I say what I've always said. *See you Monday bright and early.*

The elevator ride down is slow, and when I get home, I change into my yoga pants. I lock up my house, then grab my luggage. I don't know how long I'm going for, so I am bringing three bags. I also don't know why I'm bringing all these clothes since my plan is to be on the beach every day.

"Your car is waiting," the doorman says to me, and I smile at him.

"Have a happy holiday," I say, and he just nods his head at me.

I sit in the car, looking out the window. The holiday decorations are lit up everywhere. I watch the city fade away as we make it to the airport. The plane is waiting for me as soon as I get there.

I lied to Erika. My flight is exactly at five o'clock. I wanted to be in the air when the notice goes out. I walk up the steps, and the attendant waits for me with a glass of champagne. "Welcome aboard."

"Thank you," I say, grabbing the glass and walking into the plane. I sit down, fasten my seat belt, and nod at the attendant who closes the door.

My phone beeps with an email alert, and I look down to see that my notice is out. Bringing my glass to my lips, I say, "Goodbye," right before I take a sip.

THIRTY-FOUR

NICO

"HAVE YOU CHECKED your emails?" Lizzie asks as she walks into my office. I look up at her.

"No," I say, looking back down at the contracts on my desk. "That's what you do."

"I think you should check your email," she says, and I run my hands through my hair.

"Lizzie, I don't have time for this, nor do I want to." My eyes burn as I grab my phone and open my emails. Ever since Becca left my house, I've been in a daze of sorts. I sleep maybe three hours a night if that. I travel with the team, but to be honest, not even that is keeping my mind off her. "What am I looking for?" I ask, but the minute I see her name, I don't ask anymore questions. My heart speeds up, and for a moment, I'm happy.

From: Becca Edwards

To: Nico Harrison

A little note from Becca.

Good Afternoon,

I hope this email finds you well. I'm writing today to inform you that effective immediately, I will be on an undetermined sabbatical. It was a very hard decision to make, one that I did not do lightly. But one that I felt needed to be done.

This in no way will alter the way we do business nor will it hinder any of the contracts.

In my absence, I will be leaving you in the very capable hands of Erika Markingson. She has been my right-hand person for the past three years, and I have no doubt that you will not even miss me.

I want to take this time to wish you and your family the best holiday season.

Until next time.

Becca

"Oh my God," I say, reading it, my heartbeat finally slowing down. "Get Manning on the phone," I say, but my fingers are already dialing Manning. He sends me straight to voice mail, and it's no surprise since we have been at odds since he found out I was married. "It's me. Call me back." He made it clear whose side he was on, and it wasn't mine. "This is crazy." I get up, grabbing my jacket. "Her work is her life."

"The emails says otherwise," Lizzie says.

"Find out everything," I say, walking to the elevator. "And I mean everything."

"I'm not Sherlock Holmes." She puts her hands on her hips, and I just glare at her. "But I will make some phone calls and see if anyone knows anything." I nod at her, getting into the elevator. "Where are you going?" she asks.

"Going to the rink to see if anyone will tell me anything," I say.

"That sounds like a sane thing to do!" she shouts as the doors close.

When I walk into the rink, I see that the team is already there, which is not unusual since we are playing a game tonight. I nod to a couple of people I see, my eyes scanning the room looking for Manning.

"Hey," I say when I see him on the stationary bike. I walk closer to him, and he just looks at me. "I was looking for you."

"You found me," he says, huffing while he grabs his bottle of pre-game whatever he drinks. "What do you want?"

I look around, making sure no one is listening to our conversation. "You knew she was leaving."

He just glares at me. "What's it to you?" He shakes his head. "Where is your wife?"

I ignore the second part of his question. "You know where she went?"

"Yup," he says, stopping pedaling. "I do." He gets up and walks away from me.

"Is she okay?" I whisper, and he turns to look at me. "I just want to know if she's okay."

"She is far from okay," he hisses, his voice low as not to bring attention to us. "But hopefully, she will be." I just nod at him. I don't say anything more.

I walk out at the same time Lizzie walks in. "Where

are you going?"

"Home," I say, and she looks at me with her mouth hanging open.

"We play tonight." She points at the door I just walked out from.

"I'll watch it on the television," I say. "Did you find out anything?"

"Nothing yet." She shakes her head. "But I put out some feelers."

"Let me know," I say and walk away from her toward my car. I get home, walking straight upstairs to my room. I throw my jacket on the chair in the corner, unbuttoning the cuff links when the phone rings.

I walk out to my jacket and pull it out to see it's Laurene. "Hey." Pressing my shoulder to my ear, I hold the phone while I undress.

"It's done," she says, and I sit on the bed. "Just like it never happened." I breathe out a huge sigh of relief.

"Are you sure they won't find out?" I ask. "It would suck really hard if we went through all this for nothing."

"If anything comes up, I'm going to cry." She laughs. "No one wants to fuck with a woman who cries." I laugh. "I heard about Becca."

"Yeah," I say softly. "I don't know what to do," I say. "I don't know where to go. I feel so defeated, like there is nothing left, and I have no idea what to do with these feelings."

"I wish I had the answer," she says. "I wish that I could make it all better."

"You and me both," I say. "I'm going to take a shower

and head to bed."

"It's six." She laughs. "Aren't you going to the game?"

"Nah," I say to her. "I'm going to watch it from home."

"Okay, let me know if you need anything." I press the end button, then get up and go shower.

I don't bother watching the game. Instead, I go outside and sit down. Looking up at the stars blinking in the sky, I sit here until the sun starts to come up, my eyes never even closing once.

I walk back into the house, coming face-to-face with Lizzie and Laurene, both in their robes raiding my fridge. "What are you guys doing?" I ask, causing them to both yelp.

"You scared the shit out of me," Lizzie says, dropping the loaf of bread she was holding and putting her hand on her chest. "What the fuck?"

"Why are you up?" Laurene asks, the bag of chips in her hands squashed to her chest.

"The question is, why the fuck are you in my fridge?" I tilt my head to the side.

"I had no food," Lizzie says. "And you have food, so …"

"Have you not been to bed?" Laurene asks.

"I had things on my mind," I say.

"She's gone," Lizzie says, looking at me. "Took off to Turks."

My heart speeds up, my palms getting wet. "How do you know?"

"I ran into Francis and pretended I knew," Lizzie says.

"Told him she called me about houses."

"Did he say how long she will be gone for?" I ask, the lump coming to my throat.

"She isn't sure yet. At least for a month," she says, and I just nod at her.

"Turn off the lights when you're done," I tell them, walking back to my room. I slip into bed, thinking about Becca alone on some island.

When I wake the next day, it's after nine, and I feel like I'm hungover even though I haven't drunk anything. I walk around with a hollowness in my chest, knowing a piece of me is gone. Unless I get her back, that piece will be gone forever.

I pick up the phone and call Lizzie, who answers right away. "Do you have time?" I ask. "I want to talk to you."

She comes down a minute later. Sitting here in the living room, I tell her my plan. She wipes tears away from her cheeks and a sob comes out. "Are you sure?"

"I haven't been more sure in my whole life," I say. "I need to do this. For me. For her. For us."

"But," she says and then stops. "But …"

"But nothing. It'll be fine. It has to be fine. I love her," I say, trembling. "So much, Lizzie, I feel like I can't breathe without her. I feel a piece of me is missing, and she has that piece."

"When do you think you are going to leave?" she asks.

"Tomorrow," I say. "I just need to find out where she is, and as soon as I find out, I'll be on the next plane out."

"Francis and Trevor are the only ones who will tell

you where she is." Lizzie grabs a tissue from beside her and blows her nose. "And Manning."

"I'm going to Manning's house," I say, and she nods.

"Do you need me to come with you?" she asks, and I shake my head. She gives me a hug, and I walk to the door, getting in my car.

I pull up at Manning's, and I ring the bell. I hold my breath when I hear the lock opening. Evelyn greets me, and there is not even a smile on her face like always. "Nico."

"Hey, Evelyn, I was wondering if Manning was home?" I ask, and she takes a step back for me to walk in. Manning comes to the door and sees me. "I just need a minute of your time."

Evelyn walks over to him and holds his hand. "I know she's gone," I start talking. "And I'm going after her."

"For what?" he asks.

"Because I'm dying without her," I say. "I die a little more inside every single day that I'm not with her."

"What about Laurene?" Manning asks.

"I can't tell you what it's about, but it isn't what you think it is," I say. "You just have to trust me on that." He just watches me, and I can see his head turning. "I'm stepping away." His mouth opens. "I'm naming Lizzie my new GM."

"That team is your life," he says.

"No," I correct, "that team *was* my life."

"If she finds out I told you, she might never speak to me again," Manning says.

"Unless this is what she needs," Evelyn says.

"If you fuck her over," Manning says, "I won't give a shit who you are. I'm going to beat the shit out of you."

"If I fuck up again," I say, the pressure on my chest getting tighter, "I'll tie my hands behind me."

I walk out of there and call Lizzie. "I need a plane in an hour," I say, rushing home and packing my bags. She drives me to the plane, and when I hug her goodbye, she is softly crying.

Looking out the window after I board the plane, my mind goes all over the place as I put my speech together. The aquamarine color of the ocean surrounds me when I land. There is a car waiting for me, and when I pull up to the house, the maid lets me in. "I'm looking for Becca."

"Right in the back." She points down the marble hall-way toward the outside. I make my way outside, my eyes not even taking in everything that the house has. My only focus right is getting to Becca. I walk out, and the sun hits me right away. I put my hand over my eyes as I look into the massive backyard that leads to the beach.

A man walks back my way with a tray in his hand. "She is on the beach," he says, pointing in the direction he just came from. I walk, my heart thumping in my chest. I spot her on one of the covered canopy beds.

The soft breeze makes the curtain on the canopy flut-ter. I just watch her as she watches the ocean. She must sense someone is staring at her because she turns my way, and her face is filled with shock. She swings her legs off the canopy bed and comes to me. I take her in; she's wearing a baby blue bikini. The closer she gets to me, the more I feel alive. "What are you doing here?"

I just look at her as she pushes the hair away from her face. I had this whole speech planned out and knew everything I wanted to say. Yet right now, at the moment, the only thing that comes out are two words. "You're here."

THIRTY-FIVE

BECCA

I FEEL EYES on me and turn my head. "Nico," I whisper, and suddenly think I'm having a heatstroke. He can't be here. How is he here when only four people know where I am? I get up, my feet moving without my consent toward him. "What are you doing here?" I ask, shocked that he is actually here.

He just looks at me as if he is trying to come up with the words. The soft breeze blows my hair in front of my face. My heart is beating so hard in my chest I don't think I hear him when he says two words that rock me off my axis. "You're here."

I shake my head. "What?" The sound of the waves crashing near us seems like it's in speaker mode. The wind suddenly starts to pick up, and I wonder if it's just for us. If Mother Nature is throwing us another curveball.

He steps closer to me, his hands landing on my hips, and my whole body suddenly awakens. "You're here," he says, and his hand reaches up, and he tries to tuck the hair behind my ear. "I just …"

"You shouldn't be here," I say. "It's not …"

"There is nowhere else I belong," he says, and he looks down. "There is nowhere else I want to be." He palms my cheek with his hand. "Becca." When he says my name, I try to stop myself from feeling anything. I try to stop myself from giving in to him. I try so hard, but my heart has other ideas. "I don't know if I can say any words that will make you forgive me." The tears start to come as well as the lump in my throat. "There is nothing that I can do except show you just how much I love you." My hand moves up to my cheek. "I don't even know how to do this. I had this whole speech planned. A whole declaration of love that I was going to say. Yet with one look at you, I've forgotten everything."

"Nico," I say through the lump in my throat.

"When you left me, my heart stopped," he says, and I can feel his nervousness through his touch. "I felt empty. I felt hollow. I felt nothing." I swallow instead of saying anything. I don't think I could say anything, to be honest. "Every single day, I would wait for something to happen. I would wake, hoping that today I would feel something, but nothing came." His forehead goes down to mine. "My heart started beating again when I saw you just now. It's as if I was brought back to life."

"I don't know what to say," I answer honestly.

"Let me stay," he says. "Let me stay and prove to you that I will put you first every single time. Let me stay and show you what you mean to me." His voice dips low.

"Please, Becca."

"I know how you feel," I finally say, trying to say the words without my voice shaking, but I fail miserably. "I've been here in paradise," I say. "Waking every day, hoping the pain stops. I wake every single day, hoping you will be here, and this will all be a terrible nightmare." I lick my lips, the tears flowing like a river downstream. "Every single day." My voice cracks.

"Becca." I know he wants to kiss me, but he's stopping because he's waiting for me to make the move. Making sure I'm okay with all of this. "I'm not going anywhere, not this time. Not ever." There is so much to talk about, so much to discuss, but all that slips my mind when I take one step forward, closing the little distance between us.

"Nico," I say his name again, but all the words are gone except for the next two words. "Kiss me."

I don't even finish the last word before his lips crash on mine. His other hand comes up to my face the same time his tongue slips into my mouth. In all of my dreams, there is always him kissing me. In all of my dreams, I feel his hands on me. But nothing and I mean nothing could compare to this kiss.

My arms go around his neck as I push my body into his. We both moan into each other's mouth. "Nico," I say breathlessly, letting go of his lips. My inner body groans. His hands fall from my face. "Come with me." I hold out my hand to him, and he grabs it, his fingers slipping into mine.

"We have so much to talk about," I say as I lead him

back to my bedroom. "There is just so much."

"How many people are staying here?" he asks, looking up at the massive house, and I laugh.

"It's just us," I say as I walk toward my bedroom. Slipping off the path into my bedroom, the cold air hits me right away. "Welcome," I say.

I don't say anything because he grabs me, his mouth coming back to mine. "Later," he says, taking his mouth off mine. "I'm going to enjoy this bikini more," he says. "But for now, I just want to make love to you."

I smile at him. "Then what are you waiting for?" I say, and he grabs me around the waist. The kiss is soft and slow, as he walks me backward toward the bed.

He picks me up at my waist and lays me on the middle of the bed. He looks down at me. "I've prayed for this moment since you left," he says, pulling off his T-shirt. "I would have made deals with the devil to get you back," he says, and I know the feeling. I know all of this because I would have done the same. I would have given everything I had to go back to the last time I was with him. I would have given everything just for one more minute with him.

He comes down on me, and my legs wrap around his waist as he kisses my neck, sucking in softly. My eyes close as my back arches up when he switches sides. "Nico," I whisper, my nails scratching down his back. His tongue trails up to my mouth, my tongue coming out to meet his. He gets up on his knees, his hand going to my chest right on top of my beating heart.

"You own me," he says, looking into my eyes. "Every

single piece of me is yours." He unbuttons his pants with his one free hand. "I'm yours."

I move my hands to my hips and the two little bows keeping my bikini bottoms intact. I untie them and my bikini bottom falls open. "I'm yours," I say, "heart, body, and soul." I sit up and kiss where his heart is, pulling down his pants from his hips. I lie back down as he takes his cock into his hand and rubs up and down my slit. We both watch as he enters me, moaning when he gets all the way in. He falls on top of me with his elbows on either side of my head. Our eyes lock on each other as he thrusts into me over and over again.

It's almost as if our eyes are making a memory of this moment. Our lips on top of each other's but not touching. I wrap my legs around him even tighter, not willing to let him go. "I love you," he says to me over and over again.

My back arches into him as I come, and he follows me. He falls on me, and I welcome his weight. My hands go to his hair as he buries his face in my neck. "I love you," I say to him, and I feel his soft kisses on my neck.

He wraps his arm around my waist, picking me up with him. "Time for a nice shower," he says, and I just wrap my arms around his neck as he walks to the shower. He spots the tub. "Or a bath."

"We can just go in the pool if you'd like," I say as he places me on the counter.

"I have to have you again," he says, and I just watch him as he walks to the tub and starts the water, his pants hanging on his hips. "And I'm not doing it in the pool."

"How long can you stay?" I ask, and I know that I shouldn't be bringing it up yet since he just got here. But I have to prepare myself to be without him again.

"As long as you want me here," he says, and I smile.

"I want you to stay all the time, but I know that you have a team to get back to." He shakes his head, and I just look at him.

"I left it," he says three words that if I wasn't sitting would have knocked me on my ass.

"What do you mean, you left it?" I ask for clarification.

"Lizzie is the new GM," he says, pulling down his pants and boxers in one fluid motion. "I still own the team, but I'm not going to be involved that much."

"But …" I say the word. "But you love that team."

"I do." He comes to me. "I love that team." He kisses my lips. "But I love you more, and I choose myself before the team."

"Laurene," I say. "This isn't going to hurt her, is it?"

He blinks and laughs. "Another reason you are too good for me." He kisses me softly. "Instead of thinking about you, you are thinking about everyone else."

"I'm thinking about you," I finally tell him. "I'm thinking that you couldn't live with yourself and the guilt if you didn't fulfill a promise," I say.

"The marriage was annulled yesterday," he says, and I don't think he could shock me more. "Not sure if the press picked it up or not, and we don't care. If the company takes back their sale, it will look bad on them."

"I can't believe all this," I say the truth. "That you are

here. That you came for me. That you are single. It's just so much."

"Well, good news." I reach behind me and pull on the string to make my bikini top fall. "I can spend the rest of my life showing you that it's real."

THIRTY-SIX

Nico

MY EYES FLICKER open, and I look over at the empty bed. I just lie here with the bright sun beaming and the blue turquoise water in the distance. I don't think I could ever tire of this view. I hear the toilet flush, then turn to see her walking out of the bathroom. Her hair is hanging loose, her skin looking sun-kissed. "Good morning." She crawls into bed with me, and my cock stirs awake. She leans down and kisses my lips. "Hi," she says softly, putting her hands right by my head.

"Hi," I say, pushing the sheet off me so my cock can come out. "When did you wake up?" I ask, my hands going from her hips, slowly moving up to her tits. Her nipples pebble when I roll them between my thumb and forefinger.

"Not too long ago," she says, sitting up just a touch and reaching in behind her for my cock. She lines it up and slowly slides down my cock. The both of us close our eyes. "I have to say." She puts her hands on my chest as she slides up and down. "I like to wake up with your face between my legs." She smirks at me as she moves all the way up and slams down on my cock.

"I can arrange that." I watch her as she rides me. "So wet for me." I lick my thumb and find her clit. "You like that, don't you?" I can feel her pussy getting tighter and tighter as I play with her. "I'm almost there."

"Me, too," she pants out and I wait for her to come before holding her hips in my hands and slamming her down on me as I come inside her.

"Now that was a good morning wake-up call." I slap her ass as she collapses on top of me. I roll her over to the side and slide out of her to go to the bathroom.

I've been here for over two weeks, and I don't regret it even for one second. The days are spent with us lounging around in this massive house. You can always find us wrapped up in each other's arms. I'm pretty sure the staff thinks we are nymphomaniacs because they've caught us daily in some phase of undress.

"Do you want to head down to the beach and have breakfast?" she asks, and when I walk back into the room, she is putting on another bikini. I swear I have her every hour I'm awake, and it's still not enough. "Stop looking at me like that."

"Like what?" I ask with a smirk as I walk over to grab a pair of shorts.

"Like I'm the one you'll be having for breakfast." She laughs, slipping her feet into flip-flops. "We gave the girl a heart attack yesterday when she came back to collect the plates, and you had me spread on the table."

"That"—I point at her—"was your fault. You bent over beside my chair. It was either fuck you bent over or have dessert." I wink at her, and we walk out to one of the shaded areas. "I found your thong." I laugh, bending down and picking up her thong I ripped off her last night on our way back from having her on the beach. I put it in my pocket. "This wouldn't happen if you'd just listen to me."

"About what?" she asks, smiling at the lady who nods at us and pours us two glasses of orange juice as we sit at the massive table that seats twenty-six people.

"It's a waste to wear panties. I told you that after day one." I lean over and kiss her neck. We keep our hands to ourselves during breakfast, but the minute we get back into the room, I want her naked again. This time, it lasts longer. I take my time with her, making her come and beg over and over again. When I finally flip her over and grab her hips, I slide into her so hard I move the bed again. I finally come with her name on my lips.

"When does the sex stop being good?" she asks, looking over at me when I walk back into the room. "Like it was good at the beginning, you know. We are both hot for each other. Then it was supposed to, I don't know, simmer down, but …"

"But all you want is more cock," I say. She gets up, and she has my finger marks on her hips and her thighs. She also has two bite marks on each breast.

"Let's go sit on the beach," she says as she slips on another bikini bottom and top.

We walk past the pool and head for the beach. "This is so beautiful." She grabs my hand, and we head to the water. It's serene, and we walk in the calm waters. I grab her as she wraps her legs around my waist. "I'm going to miss this." She wraps her arms around my shoulders. Neither of us says anything as we kiss, our kisses tasting salty. "I need you," she says when I suck her ear. I walk out of the water with her legs wrapped around me the whole time.

I carry her to the shower, where I give her what she asked for. She gets out of the shower before me, and when I towel-dry myself and walk out of the room, she is sitting on the bed dressed with our luggage packed beside her. I stop in my tracks. "What is going on?"

She takes a deep breath, and I'm suddenly nervous she is going to tell me something I don't want to hear. "We are going back home." I just look at her as she gets up. "I know that you gave up everything for me." She stands in front of me. "And I can't tell you how much that meant to me. To be put first before anything and anyone."

"I'd do it every single day for the rest of my life," I say. "Walking away from that for you was the easiest decision of my life."

"Well, I'm giving it back to you," she says. "The plane is waiting for us and is going to bring us straight to Philly. The team has a game tomorrow, and we are going to be there."

"But …" I say, and I stop thinking if I should tell her my fears or not.

"But what?" she asks.

"But what if you hate it? What if you hate me working and not spending all my time with you?" I finally say out loud.

"Oh, dear God." She rolls her eyes. "I'm not going to lie. These past couple of weeks have been amazing and simply the best time of my life, but we need a break from each other."

"Are you sick of me already?" I joke with her, and she shakes her head. "So we go back home and then what?"

"And then we get back to work." She finishes the sentence. "I don't know how much work I am going to have, to be honest."

"Where are you going to live?" I ask, and she tilts her head. "If we go back, I'm not going to be without you."

"What are you saying?" she asks.

"Rule number one, you move in with me," I say. "Not really sure it's up for discussion because if you don't move in with me, I'm moving in with you."

"So I don't get a say in this." She puts her hands on her hips.

"You get to decide where we live. Your place or mine," I say.

"Travel," she says. "You are going to travel with the team."

"Not if it's more than one day," I say, and she rolls her eyes. "Unless you meet me there after the second day."

"We can check our schedules and make it work." She gives in to that one.

"One more thing," I say, walking over to my carry-on bag that I dumped on the chair two weeks ago, and it hasn't moved since. I reach inside and grab out the red box I bought before I boarded the plane. "You do it with my ring on your finger." She gasps out when I get down on one knee and open the box.

"Are you really doing this naked?" she asks, and I laugh.

"I was going to do this tomorrow with candles and roses and all of that, but you changed the plans on me." I laugh. "Becca, I didn't believe in love before you," I say. "I didn't know what love was, and then one day, I looked over at you, and it was like a kick in the stomach." She laughs, wiping away tears. "You were there all along, and then when I lost you, I knew that I would never be the same without you. I knew that you were the only one for me. Will you marry me and grow old with me?"

"I want kids," she says, and I shake my head.

"Only you would have a counteroffer to a marriage proposal," I say. "We can have kids."

"I don't want any nannies either," she says.

"Whatever you want," I say.

"Okay," she says softly. "I'll marry you." She bends down to kiss me, holding my face in her hand. She turns around before I slip the ring on her finger.

"Where are you going?" I ask, and she grabs her phone.

"Changing the plans. We can leave tomorrow afternoon and make it to Philly for the game." I just watch her. "Um, you just asked me to marry you. We have to celebrate and have all the sex." She tosses down the phone, coming over to me.

"Will you let me put the ring on you now?" I ask, and she holds out her shaky left hand. I take out the five-carat princess-cut diamond with round pink diamonds in the band. It fits on her hand perfectly; she doesn't even take a second to look at it. Instead, she gets down on her knees in front of me.

"Will you marry me?" she asks, and I laugh. "You didn't think that you would ask me, and I don't ask you." She slips her shirt over her head.

"Just remember." I pull her to me, slipping off her pants and laying her on the floor. "I asked you first," I say, sliding into her.

EPILOGUE ONE

Becca

"Where are you taking me?" I ask as I get into his SUV. "I just want to go home."

"It's just a small detour," he says, and I look in the back at Lizzie, who just snorts. We just got back from a one-week road trip, and I have to say, I'm so over it. I tried to get out of it, but let's just say he won that argument.

"Are you hungry?" he asks, and I shake my head.

"I'm tired," I say. "I want a bath and my bed."

We pull up to a house as he parks in the driveway. "Where are we?" I ask, getting out of the car and looking at the house. It's two stories, and the bright lights show me the white with black windows and doors. I look over at Nico as he walks to me and kisses my lips. He does that often. I could be talking to someone, and he will just come over to kiss me. When we got back from the island, the news of his annulment had died down, so no one really cared. Then when Laurene announced that she was married to Lizzie, that was a bigger news story than her annulment. Needless to say, she finally took over her father's company, and it's thriving. She travels an insane amount, but they spend at least three weeks a month together. So Lizzie is flying to her most of the time.

He looks over at Lizzie, who just hands him a set of keys. "Thank you," he says, and we walk up the concrete pathway to the front door. The light is on in the hallway, and we see the winding staircase, but it's only two stories. The marble hallway looks so shiny. "Let me show you the kitchen," he says with excitement.

We walk past a dining room and then come to the open concept family room and massive kitchen with the biggest island I've ever seen. "Nico, whose house is this?" I ask, and he turns around.

"It's ours." He shocks me, and I just look at him. "What do you think?"

"This should be fun," Lizzie says from behind me, coming in and grabbing a stool from under the counter.

"I don't understand," I say, looking at him confused.

"You hate my house," he says to me.

"I don't hate your house," I say. "I just …"

"You hate his house," Lizzie says, and I turn to glare at her. "What? Just last week, you came down the steps cursing about his house," she reminds me.

"I called him for ten minutes straight, and he didn't hear me," I argue back.

"You were yelling at him from the west wing," Lizzie says.

"I could have been lying on the floor dying, and no one would have heard me." I put my hands on my hips. "Besides, who has a house that big for one person?"

"Um, I live there also." She puts up her hand.

"Anyway," Nico says, tired of us going back and forth. "You hate my house, and you always say how you want a home."

"So you bought me a house." I look at him. "Without talking to me about it."

"Let me show you the bedrooms," he says, ignoring the last part I just said.

"Good luck," Lizzie says. "Actually, I'm going home." She gets up. "See you guys tomorrow." She walks out with her hand up to wave goodbye, grabbing the car keys on her way out.

He grabs my hand and pulls me up the stairs and toward the end of the hall to the master bedroom. "There are only three bedrooms."

"We are only two people who use one bedroom," I say, and he just looks over at me.

"You have a whole bedroom full of clothes," he reminds me.

"I would move them into your room, because you have ten empty bedrooms," I remind him. "So." He just laughs.

I look around the big bedroom with a king-size bed and white bench in front of it. "I can't," I say, walking to check out the average-size bathroom. "You bought this without even talking to me."

"I want you to feel at home," he says, putting his

hands in his pockets. "And if you were to faint, I could hear you in this house."

"I want to contribute to the house so it's ours," I say, and he just laughs and looks down. "I'm serious, Nico."

"Becca, I don't give a shit what you have to say, you aren't paying a penny for this house. You need to come back with another proposal."

"Fine," I say. "I pick out the nursery colors."

"Fine," he says, and then he stops to look at me as I blink away tears. "Wait." He finally sees me. "What are you saying?"

"Well," I say. "I'm sort of late." I finally blurt out the little secret that I've been holding in for a week.

"I don't understand," he says, and I tilt my head.

"Well, I was supposed to get my period last week," I start to explain, and he rolls his eyes, "and I didn't."

"But …" He points at me. "I see you take your pill."

"Yes," I say, "but I was also sick last month, and I told you that the antibiotics I was taking recommended we use additional protection."

He pffts out. "I'm not wearing a condom with you."

"Well, and we are in a predicament because you didn't want to wrap up." I put my hands on my hips.

"Can it happen that easily?" he asks, and I gawk at him.

"We have sex five times a day; it's not just a slip one day. Do you know how much sperm that is?" I say. "Trust me, I know. I googled it."

"Well, how do we find out?" he asks, and I look over at him, walking to my purse and taking out the pregnancy test I bought at the pharmacy right before getting on the plane with him.

"I have to pee on the stick." I hold up the box.

I turn and walk to the bathroom and feel him right behind me. "Um, no, you stay out here."

"I've been in there." He laughs, and I push him out, closing the door and locking it.

I pee on the stick and put it down on the counter, walking out to the bedroom. I see him sitting on the bed. "Are you mad?" I ask, worried that he is in more than he wants to be. "I know that this is fast, and I know we haven't discussed this in detail, so I want you to know that if you aren't ready, I get it. But I'm going to have this baby regardless, and I want you to know I can do it on my own if need be." I try not to sob out the last part. For the past five days, I've been so fucking emotional it's been exhausting just trying not to cry at every fucking thing.

"Are you insane?" he says, and he holds out his hand to me. I walk over, and he puts his hands on my hips as he looks up at me. "I want to marry you," he says, "and have babies with you. The only thing is, if you're pregnant, we are getting married tomorrow."

"What?" I ask, shocked.

"My child is in you," he says.

"People have babies without being married, Nico," I say.

"We get married, you get the nursery choice," he says, and I tilt my head.

"Last name hyphenated?" I ask. I wait to see his reaction, and I laugh. "I was kidding on that one." I look down. "I'm scared," I finally tell him. "I'm scared that I'll be disappointed if I'm not."

"So if you're not, we continue to try until you are," he says just like that. "Do you want me to come with you?" he asks, and I nod.

Together, we walk into the bathroom where the white test sits on the counter. "Here goes nothing," I say, picking it up and seeing two lines. I look back at him. "We're going to have a baby."

EPILOGUE TWO

Nico

Three years later

"DID YOU TELL Phoenix he could come on the plane with you?" I look over at my wife as she stands there, rubbing her pregnant belly. She's five months pregnant, and unlike Phoenix, this pregnancy is kicking her ass. She started getting morning sickness the minute she found out she was pregnant.

"I said that I would talk to Mommy," I say, getting up from my office chair and walking over to her. She rolls her eyes. I try not to laugh because I actually said I would talk to Mommy, but then I also told him that Mommy would say yes.

"You can't just take him on the plane to take him for a ride. It's not the same as a car," she points out, and I shrug.

"Um, he said dada airplane, and then he smiled at me.

How was I supposed to say no?" I say. "How can I say no to that?" I put my hands on her belly.

"Easy," she says. "No. See how I just did it. Like, Becca, do you want to have sex tonight? No."

I laugh because if sex with Becca was hot before, it's on another level while she's pregnant. She jumps on me every time I walk in the room, and I love every minute of it. "You lie," I whisper, kissing her neck. "So if I bent you over right now," I whisper in her ear, "raised your dress, and slipped into you"—I nip at her earlobe—"you would say no?"

"That's not fair. I haven't seen you in two days." I was in New York and then Philly. Our team is at the top of the standings, and if all goes well, I will be bringing the Cup to Dallas. The one piece I've been after for the past three years. It's so close I can taste it.

"See? Not so easy to say no, is it?" I say, and she shakes her head. Our son comes back into the room with his sippy under his arm.

He looks like a mix of both of us. "Dada." He holds up his arms.

"Traitor," my wife says to him, and he smiles and puts his head on my shoulder. "I named you."

"Trust me, I would never try to take that away from you," I say.

"It's only fair. He was conceived in Phoenix," she says, and I laugh.

"I'm pretty sure that baby was conceived in the pool," I say, and she laughs. "We are not naming her Whirl-pool."

"If this baby comes out a boy, we need to have another kick-ass name," she says.

"Well, you know I get to name the next one," I say. "It's in our agreement."

"That can be tossed out," she says. "I married you in a pantsuit."

I laugh, and Phoenix copies me. "She's funny, isn't she." I kiss her. "Go get washed up. I'll put him to bed and join you. Be naked," I say.

"Naked," Phoenix says and starts to lift his shirt.

"Not you, buddy," I say, walking out of our bedroom and to his nursery. I sit in the rocking chair as I read to him. He falls asleep in no time, and I put him down.

I look around at the nursery that my wife painted. She did everything. She is hands-on with our son, and to this day, we've had a babysitter maybe five times. But we both wanted it this way.

The phone beeps in my pocket, and I take it out and press the green button. "Hello," I say.

"Nico." I hear a man say my name. "It's Cooper Grant."

"Hey," I say to him. "How are you?"

"I'm good. Just getting on the plane," he says, and I smile.

"Well," I say, "Cooper Grant, welcome to Dallas."

"It's going to be something crazy," he says, little does he know. "I just hope that it's not my Only One Regret!"

www.ingramcontent.com/pod-product-compliance
Lightning Source LLC
Chambersburg PA
CBHW072045190726

48294CB00005B/1412